# CANYON
## OF
# DANGER

**Goldtown Adventures Series**

*Badge of Honor*
*Tunnel of Gold*
*Canyon of Danger*
*River of Peril*

GOLDTOWN ADVENTURES #3

# CANYON
## OF
# DANGER

## SUSAN K. MARLOW

**Kregel**
*Publications*

*Canyon of Danger*
© 2013 by Susan K. Marlow

Illustrations © 2013 by Melissa McConnell

Published by Kregel Publications, a division of Kregel Inc., 2450 Oak Industrial Dr. NE, Grand Rapids, MI 49505.

ISBN 978-0-8254-4296-4

Printed in the United States of America
19 20 21 22 23 24 25 / 7 6 5 4 3

# Contents

# ⤚≼ CHAPTER 1 ≽⤙

# Man of the Family

GOLDTOWN, CALIFORNIA, 1864

Jem Coulter took the back porch steps in a flying leap and nearly tore the screen door off its hinges in his eagerness to get inside the ranch house. He didn't bother to remove his hat. No time for such niceties. Not today. Not when life and death hung in the balance.

*Gotta hurry!* Jem clomped through the kitchen, where Aunt Rose stood at the huge, black cook stove. She was stirring a pot of something sweet-smelling, and Jem's mouth watered. Applesauce! Nobody could make applesauce—or anything else—like Aunt Rose. Jem figured he'd grown two inches and gained ten pounds since spring, when his aunt and cousin Nathan had moved in.

Jem had no time to beg a taste of applesauce today. He hurried into the front room and crossed over to the fireplace. The ashes lay cold and dead, just as they had all summer. No need for a fire when the unrelenting California sun beat down on the small ranch house. It kept Jem's attic loft as hot as a blacksmith's forge.

Jem reached for his father's Henry rifle, which rested on the rack above the fireplace.

"Jeremiah Isaiah!"

Aunt Rose's voice stopped Jem in his tracks. *Roasted rattlesnakes! She sure likes to hear the sound of my name.*

Jem had heard his full name more times in the past four months than in all of his twelve years put together. Mama had never called him Jeremiah unless she was really aggravated at him. Jem winced. He still missed his mother, even though she had been gone these past four years. Aunt Rose did a good job managing her brother's family, but it wasn't the same as when Mama was alive.

Jem turned around empty-handed. He hoped Aunt Rose would be quick. He had to get back to the herd. "Yes, ma'am?"

"What do you mean by tearing through the house like a wild Indian?" Aunt Rose stood in the doorway, a wooden spoon in one hand and her other hand planted on her hip. She was a small woman—barely up to Pa's shoulders—but Jem knew better than to cross her.

She waved the applesauce spoon at him. "Take that hat off, young man. This is a respectable home, not a saloon or a miner's shack."

Jem whipped off his hat and tossed it on the sagging couch to his left.

"Well?" his aunt demanded. "Why are you running around in this heat? Did you water the chickens and the garden? Is the wood split for tomorrow? What about that loose section of fence around the garden? Rabbits have been chewing my produce."

Jem didn't know which question to answer first. His heart hammered. There was no time to listen to Aunt Rose's scolding. He had to grab the rifle and get going.

Aunt Rose gave Jem a weak smile and let her wooden spoon drop to her side. She sighed. "Forgive me for fussing at you, Jeremiah. I'm a little anxious about keeping the place up right now."

Jem relaxed. Aunt Rose wasn't sore at him. She was only fussing because Pa was gone, like Miss Cluck ruffling her feathers when something upset her. The likeness between Aunt Rose and his sister Ellie's favorite setting hen made Jem smile. "Ellie took care of the chickens hours ago," he said. "Nathan's splitting wood. I'll check the fence as soon as I can."

Aunt Rose might be uneasy about Pa leaving town on sheriff business, but Jem could hardly contain his excitement. *Pa left me in charge of the ranch!*

"I've got no choice but to escort this particular prisoner to Sacramento," Pa had explained at supper three nights ago. "I'm afraid this is the downside of being a sheriff. I hate leaving you all, but Jem's old enough to be the man of the family for a couple of weeks."

Jem felt ten feet tall at Pa's words.

"And with Nathan and Ellie to help out," Pa finished, "I've no worries. If you get in a bind, you can ask Strike to lend a hand."

Aunt Rose had made a face and clucked her tongue at the mention of Strike-it-rich Sam. "I'm sure no one will be able to drag him away from his gold claim," she'd sniffed. Her expression gave away the fact that she did not want the old prospector anywhere near the Coulter ranch.

Pa had laughed. The whole family knew Aunt Rose's low opinion of the miner. But Strike-it-rich Sam was the Coulters' best friend. If the need arose, Jem knew he could count on Strike.

Jem turned his attention back to the rifle, the rest of his aunt's questions forgotten. He carefully lifted the heavy weapon down from the rack and checked the loading tube. There were only three cartridges. He'd have to find more ammunition and maybe a small grub sack to take with him. It might be a long afternoon and evening.

Aunt Rose sucked in her breath. "Land sakes, Jeremiah! Put that thing away. You've no call to be toting around a firearm." She took a step back and regarded the long-barreled rifle as if it were a striking rattlesnake. "You heard me. Put it up."

Jem clenched his jaw to keep from talking back, but he did not return the rifle to the rack. He couldn't. Pa had left him in charge, and Jem had a job to do. Aunt Rose had lived in Goldtown for months now, but she still hadn't adjusted to the rough and wild country. *You can take Aunt Rose out of Boston,* he mused, *but I reckon you can't take Boston out of Aunt Rose.*

"I've been shooting a rifle since I was nine," Jem explained. "And Pa's been teaching me his fast draw with the pistol. Didn't Uncle Frederick teach Nathan to shoot? After all, he was a captain in the army and probably shot a gun lots of times."

Aunt Rose caught her breath and turned pale.

Too late Jem realized he had brought up a sore subject. His uncle had been killed in the Battle of Gettysburg only a year ago. It probably hurt Auntie to be reminded of such a tragedy.

"No, he did not teach Nathan to shoot," Aunt Rose said before Jem could apologize. "A gun was necessary in your uncle's profession, but he found no need for such things in the city."

Jem gripped Pa's rifle tighter. "You're probably right, but there *is* need for a rifle here." He dropped his voice, just in case ten-year-old Ellie came barreling into the house right then. "I was out checking on the cattle and I found"—he swallowed—"a dead calf."

Aunt Rose gasped.

"Please don't tell Ellie," Jem hurried on. "She puts a lot of stock in our animals. Each of those calves out there has a name. I think this was Pepper, at least from what I can tell by what's left of him. He's one of the younger calves. That's probably why a wolf could take him down."

"*Wolf?*" Her voice rose in a squeak.

Jem nodded. "I'm pretty sure. They usually stick to the hills and leave the ranchers alone, but once in a while a lone wolf gets real pesky." He paused.

"And . . . ?" Aunt Rose prompted.

"He'll come back for the rest of his meal," Jem said. "I intend to be there when he does."

"That is your father's job," Aunt Rose said in a shaky voice. "You should wait until he returns."

Jem felt a flush race up his neck and burst in his cheeks. Aunt Rose didn't understand. "No, ma'am, I can't. We only have a couple dozen head of cattle. I've gotta get that wolf. Not because he killed one of Ellie's pet calves, but because those cattle are our living. Now that we've got the new bull, Pa's working hard to increase the herd. He can't afford to lose even one calf."

For a full minute, Aunt Rose didn't say anything. She chewed on her lip while her gaze flicked from the repeating rifle in her young nephew's hands to a faraway spot out the front window, then back to the gun.

Jem held his breath. Disobeying Aunt Rose would make her angry. She was a grown-up and the closest thing he now had to a mother. He needed her support if he was going to keep the herd safe from predators. He did not want to go against her. *Please, God, make her back off. But if she insists I wait for Pa, don't let her get too riled when I go after that wolf anyway.*

"Well, Jeremiah," she finally said, "I suppose your mind's made up. Short of wrestling that rifle away from you, I see no way of keeping you from protecting the Coulter cattle."

Jem let out the breath he'd been holding.

She frowned. "I don't like it. Not one bit. But seeing as you seem to have some experience with firearms, I won't stand in your way. After all, Matthew did give you charge of the ranch during his absence."

Jem carefully laid the rifle down and threw his arms around Aunt Rose. Up until today, he'd only let his aunt kiss him on the cheek or lay a friendly hand on his shoulder. He'd never felt like engulfing her in a grateful hug. But he did so now and was rewarded with a hug in return. "Thank you, Auntie. I'll do my best to get that wolf."

While Jem found more cartridges for the rifle, Aunt Rose put together a small sack of food to take along. "Don't stay out too long past dark," she warned. "I'll keep your supper warm." Then she frowned. "What do I tell Ellianna and Nathan?"

Jem slung a canteen over one shoulder. "That I'm out watching the herd. That's true enough." He plopped his hat back on his head. "I think I'll let Pa tell Ellie about Pepper getting eaten."

Jem planned to leave behind any wolf he shot. If he dragged it home, Ellie would bombard him with questions. Before long, she'd figure out that a dead wolf probably meant that it had killed first.

Jem stopped by the outside pump to give Copper a quick drink. Thankfully, Ellie was nowhere in sight, and Nathan was asleep in the shade by the woodpile. Jem left his horse and hurried into the barn to find the scabbard to carry the rifle on horseback.

When he came out, he groaned. His golden dog romped and whined, circling Copper and wagging his tail. "You can't go along," Jem said. "You'll keep a wolf from coming anywhere near its kill."

It took another five minutes to drag Nugget to the porch

and tie him up. He whined and barked until Aunt Rose found an old bone to keep him busy.

By the time Jem left the yard, it felt like hours had passed since he'd stumbled across the dead calf. What if the wolf had already returned and finished what it began the day before?

Jem nudged Copper into a lope and made a beeline to where he'd discovered the calf earlier that afternoon. He saw the brown hide and blinked back tears. Ellie wasn't the only Coulter who was fond of their livestock.

The remains of the calf lay in a clump of scrub brush and small oaks. Jem dismounted and searched the ground all the way around the kill. Sure enough, wolf tracks in the soft dirt circled the remains then headed for deeper woods.

Jem breathed a sigh of relief. He'd given the tracks only a passing glance the first time, before hightailing it home for the rifle and supplies. There was a chance something else had taken down the calf, like a cougar. The thought of a cougar made the hairs on Jem's neck stand on end. If the tracks had turned out to be a cat, he would have leaped on Copper and headed home—as fast as he could. He knew better than to tangle with a mountain lion.

Jem led Copper away from the calf and tied him up in the woods. Then he made his way back and settled down in a brushy thicket near enough to the recent kill to have a clear view. In the distance, a small herd of cattle grazed out in the open.

He took a drink from his canteen and bit into a biscuit. It was going to be a long wait. Wolves had sharp hearing and an excellent sense of smell. If the wolf even suspected an armed hunter hid nearby, it wouldn't come within howling distance.

Jem reached out and slapped at a pesky fly then kept still. Except for the sound of chattering chipmunks and the occasional cawing crow, all was quiet. There was no breeze, and the late afternoon sun baked Jem's hiding place. He propped the rifle across his knees and leaned his head back against a tree trunk.

His thoughts drifted to what Pa would say when he learned Jem had saved the herd from a predator. He imagined his father's proud grin and a friendly clap on the shoulder. "Why, Son, you need a rifle of your own." Jem grinned and settled himself more comfortably in the thicket . . . and drifted off to sleep.

When Jem jerked awake some hours later, he found dusk settling around him. The chattering had faded away; the crow was long gone. *Some hunter you are!* he scolded himself. How could he have fallen asleep? And what had awakened him?

Then he heard it—a rustling in the brush just beyond the calf's remains. Jem's senses came alive. A cold chill raced up his spine. Carefully, quietly, he gripped the rifle and rose to his knees.

## ≒ CHAPTER 2 ≒

# Wolf?

Jem blinked and tried to focus on where he'd heard the rustling sound. In spite of his abrupt awakening, he felt groggy from his unplanned nap. The sun had dipped behind the hills in the west, but no evening breeze had risen to chase away the suffocating heat. Sweat beaded his forehead.

Jem ignored the sticky drops and peered at the underbrush near the dead calf. Had the noise really come from there? He glanced toward the rangeland. The herd was gone, no doubt bedded down for the night under a grove of oak trees.

*Swish . . . crackle.* The rustling came again. Jem turned. A shadowy form, all gray and black, was creeping around in the underbrush. *The wolf!* Jem quietly worked the lever to insert a cartridge into the rifle's chamber.

The fading light made it difficult to see clearly, but Jem could tell the beast was inching its way closer. He'd been on a wolf hunt with Pa a year ago. Jem knew the wolf was more afraid of him than he was of it. All he had to do was sit tight, wait for the wolf to show itself, take aim, and pull the trigger. Pa made it look so easy.

But now, with night closing in, it sure didn't *feel* easy. Jem found it hard to keep the heavy rifle steady as he pointed it toward the rustling sound.

*Snap!* A branch broke. At the same time, a piercing howl split the air. Startled, Jem pulled the trigger before he realized the wolf's cry was coming from some distance away. The rifle shot exploded and thrust Jem backward with a yelp of surprise.

Jem hadn't meant to shoot just then, but his fingers had taken over. *Did I get it?* He heard another faraway howl. *Hang it all! I missed!* The wolf was no doubt hightailing it out of the area as fast as it could.

Just then, snapping noises in the brush made Jem's heart pound. He caught his breath and strained to listen. Maybe a wolf hadn't been prowling around. Maybe it was something else. A bobcat? A coyote? Shooting a coyote didn't bother Jem at all. One less varmint for Nugget to chase away from the henhouse.

Jem lay still until his racing heart returned to normal. When he'd recovered his wits, he sat up and readied the Henry rifle with another round—just in case he *had* shot something, and the animal was still alive. It would be out of its head with pain at being wounded.

Jem rose and began to slowly make his way from his hiding place. He wasn't sure what he'd find. He tightened his fingers around the rifle and took a few cautious steps toward where he'd aimed his shot.

Halfway across the clearing, Jem heard an agonized moaning. He froze in horror. This was no wounded coyote yipping, or the pain-filled growl of a bobcat. A moan like that could only come from one source—a person!

With a cry of alarm, Jem put down his rifle and ran. He leaped over the dead calf's remains and plunged through the underbrush, ignoring the branches that whipped his face and caught at his clothing. A limb yanked his hat off, but he didn't stop.

When he broke through the thicket, a small paint horse whinnied and sidestepped deeper into the brush. Jem barely glanced at the animal he'd mistaken for a wolf before turning his gaze to the ground. A young man, clean-shaven and with jet-black hair, lay motionless on the ground. His eyes were closed; a groan erupted from his throat.

Jem fell to his knees beside him. *Oh, God! Please let him be all right!* "I'm s-sorry," he stammered aloud. "I didn't mean to shoot. I thought you were a . . . I mean, I was shooting at a wolf that got our calf."

The man cracked his eyelids and spoke between clenched teeth. "Do I . . . look like . . . a wolf, boy?"

Jem flushed. There was no excuse for what he'd done. *"Make sure you know what you're shooting at before you pull that trigger!"* He cringed as his father's words slammed into his head. "I'm sorry," he whispered.

The wounded man tried to sit up but fell back with another groan. A dark, wet spot seeped through the fabric near the man's left shoulder.

"Lie still," Jem said. "Rest."

"Can't rest." He took a deep, shuddering breath. "Not out here. That wolf you're after would just as soon pick me over another calf."

Jem's heart took a nosedive clear to his toes. He looked at the circle of blood soaking the man's shirt. Desperate to stop the flow, Jem pulled out his pocket knife and cut away the fabric, exposing a lean, bronze shoulder. Sure enough, a dark hole showed where the bullet had entered. Blood oozed from the wound in a slow trickle.

Jem gagged, and his stomach turned over. Why did the sight of this man's blood bother him so much? He'd seen plenty of blood in his short life. Knife fights and gunfights were common in Goldtown. The violence made him grimace, but he never felt sick. Not like this. Was it because this was personal? Because *he* was the cause of it?

"Hey, boy," the man said, "it's not that bad. You just winged me. Don't go losing your supper over it."

Jem took a deep breath and shoved his disturbing thoughts to a little-used corner of his mind. The man was right. There was no time to dwell on what he'd done. Plenty of time for that later, when Aunt Rose got hold of him or when Pa returned.

Jem reached into his back pocket and yanked out his bandana. He wadded it up and stuffed it against the wound. "Hold this real tight. It will slow the bleeding."

The man clamped down on his shoulder with his good hand. He gasped and sucked in a breath.

Another guilty stab ripped through Jem's gut. *He's hurting awful bad. What do I do now?* Somehow, he had to get the stranger to safety. But how? They were a good two or three miles from the ranch. Jem couldn't leave him alone while—

"What . . . what's your name, boy?"

Jem swallowed. "J-Jem. Jem Coulter." He glanced around at the deepening shadows. It suddenly dawned on him that if a man didn't want to get shot, then he shouldn't be creeping around on other folks' land at dusk, in dark clothing. Especially in gold country, where a suspicious-looking character could be mistaken for a claim jumper and get himself shot simply for going near a miner's claim.

"By the way," Jem said, feeling stronger, "this is our range land. I didn't expect to find people out here." It didn't make him feel any better about wounding him, but at least some of the blame for the accident could be shifted to the stranger. Maybe.

The man stiffened at Jem's words but kept a smile pasted on his face. "I reckon you got a point, Jem Coulter. I'm Rafe."

"What were you—"

"Shortcut," Rafe muttered, cutting Jem off. He closed his eyes.

When no other explanation came for Rafe's twilight wanderings, Jem bit his lip. Bringing a wounded stranger to the ranch while his father was out of town was not a good idea. Aunt Rose would probably have a conniption fit. She did not like surprises, and the California gold country was full of them.

*But what else can I do?* Jem thought. *I shot him. I can't leave him out here to fend for himself.* The sun was setting fast. It was time to grab his hat, fetch the rifle and Copper, and head home.

"I need to get you back to the ranch. Do you think you can stand long enough to get on your horse? I'll help you." Jem turned his attention to the paint pony a few yards away.

"I don't plan to stay out here and bleed to death," Rafe said. He boosted himself up on his good elbow then winced and slumped back to the ground. "But my mustang went lame on me. He's as useless as I am."

Jem felt heartened by Rafe's voice. He sounded stronger, now that the shock of being shot had worn off. But he didn't look any stronger. He lay still, his face gray. The red spot on his shirt was widening by the minute, in spite of the makeshift bandage.

"I'll get my horse and be right back." Jem leaped through the brush and raced across the clearing as if a wolf were after him. Then back through the woods, where Copper stood patiently, tied to a small tree.

The chestnut horse nickered when Jem approached, but he didn't take time to return the greeting. It took two tries before his fumbling fingers loosened the reins. Jem yanked hard. Copper responded with a snort and a jerk of his head.

"Easy, boy," Jem apologized. His hands shook as he gripped the reins and led Copper back to the injured Rafe.

"I'm back," he told the motionless figure. "Let's get you up on my horse."

Rafe opened his eyes and glanced at the chestnut horse hanging over him. He gave Jem a weak smile. "I won't be much help."

"I shot you in the shoulder. There's nothing wrong with your legs."

"That's a fact, boy," Rafe replied, struggling to sit up. "But I'm feeling a mite puny from all the blood I'm losin'."

True enough.

Rafe fingered the double holster he wore. "You can lighten the load by ten pounds if you unbuckle my pistols."

Jem hadn't paid any attention to the weapons secured around the stranger's hips. But he noticed them now. Two Colt .44 pistols peeked out from their matching holsters. Without a word, Jem worked to loosen the dead weight then swung the gear up behind Copper's saddle like a set of saddlebags.

Jem returned to the task at hand and braced his feet before bending over Rafe. It would be a struggle to lift him, but he did not look like a husky man. Not like Mr. Sims. The café owner who bought Jem's frogs stood tall and round, and looked solid as a brick wall.

Jem clasped Rafe's good hand and strained to help him stand. Once he was upright, his legs seemed in good working order. Jem kept Rafe from keeling over as he led him to Copper and guided his foot into the stirrup.

But even with Rafe's small, wiry build, Jem was breathing hard by the time he steadied him in the saddle. Rafe held the saddle horn in a white-knuckled grip.

In a flash, Jem found his hat. Then he snatched up Pa's rifle and slipped it into the scabbard.

"My horse," Rafe whispered.

Jem grabbed the mustang's reins, then mounted Copper

behind Rafe. A lame, faltering pony would slow them down, but Rafe was right. They couldn't leave the poor animal to wander around out here. A man had to care for his horse, and this one needed doctoring.

Jem scooted forward into the saddle and took up Copper's reins. It was a tight fit, sharing the saddle with another person. Occasionally, Jem and Ellie shared a saddle, but he didn't like it. He didn't like it now, either.

Rafe slumped forward but continued to grip the saddle horn. Jem slipped an arm around his waist to steady him and secured the pony's reins to the horn. Then he nudged Copper into an easy lope, one that would not push the injured pony too hard.

His thoughts whirled as Copper's pace ate up the few short miles back to the ranch. He didn't know what Rafe was doing out here, at dusk, in the middle of the vast rangeland. A shortcut, he'd said, but a shortcut to *where*? Was he prospecting for a new gold strike? Miners like Strike-it-rich Sam often left their current claims and took off looking for fresh possibilities, especially in the summertime.

*Rafe doesn't look like any gold miner I've ever seen,* Jem decided. His shiny black hair and bronze skin reminded Jem of the few Yokut or Miwok Indians he'd occasionally seen. *But Rafe speaks English as well as I do.*

"So, what were you doing out there?" Jem asked, keeping his voice light and friendly. Perhaps Rafe felt more like talking now.

"Taking . . . a walk," came the muffled answer.

Jem frowned. "Taking a walk" sounded mighty close to "None of your business."

He tried again. "I was just wondering—"

"Let it go, boy."

Jem felt a hot flush go up his neck. All right, then. He would change the subject. "Seen any wolf sign around?"

Rafe grunted. "Besides the dead calf?"

Jem fumed. The stranger was playing with him, not taking him seriously at all. He pulled Copper to a rough stop. He suddenly didn't care if Rafe's shoulder was jarred into bleeding heavily. "Listen, Mr. Rafe—"

"It's just Rafe."

"Whatever your name is," Jem snapped. "I sure didn't mean to shoot you. I heard that ol' wolf howl, and the branches snapped, and I"—he shrugged—"I got startled. I really wanted to get that wolf before it goes after another calf."

Rafe didn't reply.

"Anyway, I'm sorry I shot you, and I didn't mean to poke my nose in your business." Even if it really *was* his business, what with Pa off escorting that prisoner to Sacramento.

No answer.

For an instant, Jem wanted to shove the man off Copper, untie the mustang's reins, and gallop away. *So long, stranger!* Didn't Rafe recognize a true apology when he heard one? *Ornery, good-for-nothin' Indi—* He caught himself just in time. *Forgive me, Lord,* he prayed. *Rafe's got a right to be angry. I reckon I'd be pretty riled if somebody shot me.*

Jem tightened his grip on the reins and urged his horse forward. "We're almost home." He wouldn't say another word. Not even if it choked him. He'd let Rafe stay as angry as he wished.

A few minutes later, Rafe sighed. "Sorry, Jem. I'm not usually so short-tempered. I hurt, and I took it out on you. Listen. You get me fixed up and . . . and I won't hold shooting me against you."

As quickly as it had come, Jem's annoyance dissolved. He nodded. "Sure thing, Rafe."

The sun had sunk even lower by the time Jem saw the outbuildings of the Coulter ranch come into view. He eased

Copper into the yard and pulled him around to stop in front of the barn. "Can you dismount? It won't be long now. You can rest while I fetch the doctor."

Jem untied the pony and carefully slipped from Copper's back so he wouldn't jar Rafe. Then he glanced up. Rafe's face looked ghostly pale against the fading light. "Rafe? Can you—"

Rafe began to slide off the horse. Jem caught him, and they both toppled to the ground with a loud *thunk*.

## CHAPTER 3

# Helping Hands

"Rafe!" Jem untangled himself and stood up. He stared down at the unconscious man. The wadded-up bandana had fallen off during the ride home, and blood was pooling where he lay in a heap next to Copper. Jem didn't need to be told that Rafe needed Doc Martin right away. He turned and ran for the ranch house.

Nugget whined and lurched against his rope leash. Jem rushed past, grateful his dog was still tied up. Nugget didn't like strangers. Jem slammed through the back door and into the kitchen. "There's an injured man out back! I gotta fetch Doc Martin."

For once, Aunt Rose did not scold Jem about taking off his hat, or insist he slow down and lower his voice. Instead, she shot up from the table, where she, Nathan, and Ellie were finishing a late supper. "What happened?"

Jem paused and bit his lip. Must he tell what he did? *There's no time to explain,* came his first thought. *Let everybody think I just found him.* Awkward explanations could come later. Much later. Maybe by the time Pa came home, Rafe would be healed and gone. Then it wouldn't sound so terrible that he'd—

"I shot him," Jem blurted before he talked himself into keeping silent.

"Heaven preserve us!" Aunt Rose turned pale and clapped a hand over her mouth. She backed up against the sink, eyes wide with shock.

"It was an accident," Jem tried to explain. "I heard what I thought was the wolf and—"

"*What* wolf?" Ellie leaped up and grabbed her brother's sleeve. "You're hunting a wolf? What'd it do? Did it kill a—"

Jem shoved Ellie's hand away. "Hush!" Most of the time, he could count on Ellie to stand by him. She never tattled, and Jem usually didn't mind when she tagged along after him. She could pan gold as well as he could and catch just as many frogs to sell to the café.

But sometimes—like right now—she could be a real bother. "Hang it all, Ellie. I don't have time to explain. Rafe's out there bleeding from a shoulder wound. We need to get him settled and then go for the doctor." He turned to his cousin. "Can you help me carry him inside? He's out there, lying in the dirt."

Nathan jumped up to lend a hand, but Aunt Rose stepped in. "You'll have to settle him in the barn, Jeremiah." Her voice shook, but color had returned to her cheeks. "I won't bring a stranger—wounded or otherwise—into this house. Not with your father gone." Her dark gaze made it clear there would be no arguing.

Aunt Rose was right. Rafe needed a quiet spot to rest and recover, but with Pa gone, the house was not the right place. The barn would do just as well as a lumpy couch in the front room. Better, in fact. For the past month, Jem had been sleeping in the barn most nights. It was cooler than the loft. He'd tried to talk Nathan into moving out of their furnace of an attic, but so far his cousin had not made the switch.

"We can settle him in my spot out in the barn," Jem said.

"But hurry! I want to go after Doc Martin before it gets too dark to see my way to town."

Before Jem had finished speaking, Ellie was out the door and clattering down the porch steps. Nathan scurried after her, leaving Jem alone with his aunt.

"Oh, Jeremiah," Aunt Rose said sadly, "this is a terrible turn of events. I want a full accounting as soon as this man is tended."

Jem nodded. "Yes, ma'am, but I think he'll be all right. It's just a flesh wound. Nothing the doctor can't fix. He'll take out the bullet and slap a bandage on it." He kept his voice light. It wouldn't do to upset his aunt more than she already was.

Aunt Rose sighed, long and deep. "I'll get my basket and join you." She headed to the small bedroom she shared with Ellie.

Jem hurried out the door. From the porch he could see Ellie and Nathan squatting beside Rafe. "Don't touch him!" Jem hollered. He ran down the steps and joined them at the wounded man's side.

"He wouldn't know it if we did," Nathan said, sitting back on his heels.

Ellie glanced up at her brother. "He doesn't look too good, Jem. Do you think he'll bleed to death?"

"From a bullet in the shoulder? Hardly. Don't be a goose." He didn't admit that he was worried about the same thing. He nudged Nathan. "Help me carry him into the barn."

Rafe was not big, but his limp body was heavy and awkward. Ellie lifted one leg, and Nathan the other. Jem grasped the man under his arms, and they all lifted at once.

In the end, however, they did more dragging than carrying. Ellie tripped, and Rafe's leg hit the ground. Nathan staggered, but caught himself. Then Jem stumbled and almost dropped his share of the load.

They were all panting by the time they lowered Rafe onto the thick pile of straw Jem had turned into a bed. A heavy quilt kept the straw from poking Rafe in the back, and Ellie propped his head on Jem's goose-down pillow. In the heat, he needed no coverings.

Aunt Rose appeared just then, carrying her basket of herbs, potions, clean rags, and anything else she needed in a pinch. A precious safety pin, a match, a pencil stub . . . even a lemon drop might find its way into her collection. Jem always marveled at the jumble of odds and ends his aunt could tuck away in her small wicker basket.

She set the basket down and quickly put Ellie to work. "Fill a basin with water and bring it here. Jeremiah, help me remove his shirt. Let's see how badly he's hurt."

"Can't Nathan do it?" Jem protested. "I need to go after Doc Martin." He was itchy to be on his way.

Nathan took off running at Jem's words. "I'll put up his horse!" He was out the barn door before Jem could stop him.

Aunt Rose clucked her tongue. "You're all worked up, Jeremiah. Settle down and help me. A minute more won't make a difference."

Jem couldn't settle down, at least not on the inside. Each minute he delayed meant Rafe might lose more blood. But he crouched beside Rafe and began doing what his aunt asked.

"Hold him up while I get the rest of his shirt pulled away," Aunt Rose said. "There. Now, lay him back, but gently. Yes, that's right."

Aunt Rose's matter-of-fact orders quieted Jem's jitters. She might not enjoy the rough life in Goldtown, but after the first shock, she did not shrink back from doing what had to be done.

Jem was suddenly glad for Auntie's bossy, take-over ways. He liked strutting around as man of the family—bossing Ellie and Nathan, watching out for the livestock, and even going after a wolf. But he did *not* want to be responsible for taking care of this injured man. What if . . . what if he *died?*

"How did you manage to get him up on the horse?" Aunt Rose asked, interrupting Jem's worried thoughts.

"He was conscious, so he could give me a little help. And he doesn't weigh much." He tossed Rafe's blood-soaked shirt aside.

Ellie peered over Jem's shoulder. "He looks bad off. Just like a scrawny, plucked chicken."

"Shhh," Jem said. "You don't want him to hear you talking like that."

Aunt Rose dipped a rag in the pan of water, wrung it out, and wiped away some of the blood. More oozed out to take its place. She pressed the cloth over the swollen wound. "He's lost a great deal of blood, no doubt from jouncing around on the back of a horse."

"Doesn't look like he's got much to spare," Ellie said. "He's skinny as—"

"Ellianna," Aunt Rose warned.

Ellie pressed her lips together and kept quiet. For the moment, anyway. Ellie couldn't stay quiet for long. After all, how often did a wounded, bleeding young man show up on the ranch?

With his shirt off, Jem could make out the outline of Rafe's ribs. He didn't look starved or underfed—certainly not like a scrawny, plucked chicken. He was just lean to the point of carrying no extra weight on his body. A larger, huskier man might walk all the way to town with his shoulder shot up and dripping blood. But not this young fellow.

"There is no exit wound," Aunt Rose said, "so the bullet is still in there. You'd best ride to town now and ask Dr. Martin to come out."

Jem's errand slammed into his mind, and he shot to his feet.

"It's getting dark," Aunt Rose said. "I don't want you going to town alone."

"I'll go," Ellie said, eyeing Jem.

Aunt Rose frowned and opened her mouth to reply, but she didn't get far.

"Nathan should stay with you, Auntie, what with this strange fellow here an' all. You and me are just a lone woman and a girl. It's best I go with Jem and let Nathan stay and protect you."

Nathan had settled Rafe's pony in an empty stall and was leaning against a post, watching from a safe distance. Last spring, on his very first visit to Goldtown, Nathan's eyes had lit up at the idea of watching a knife fight. However, a trip into the hills and the sight of a bloody, injured prospector had cured Nathan of his desire to see any more such injuries.

Jem flicked his gaze from Nathan to the pale, still form lying in the hay. Aunt Rose and Ellie need not fear for their safety. Even if Rafe roused, he looked about as dangerous as a newborn kitten.

"I can go by myself," Jem said, scowling at Ellie in the dim light of the barn. He did not want his sister riding into town with him. The word "wolf" was no doubt embedded in her mind. It looked like she'd figured out a perfect way to get Jem alone.

"You'll need somebody to carry the lantern," Ellie insisted. "It'll be mighty dark on the way home."

"Doc Martin will have a lantern, so—"

"Take her along, Jeremiah," Aunt Rose said, sighing. "The two of you know that town inside out. Nathan can stay and"—she smiled at Ellie—"protect me."

"But . . ." Jem's voice trailed away when he realized he was wasting precious time arguing. It would be faster to just let Ellie tag along. Jem did not often leave the ranch after dark. A light might be a good idea. "Copper's still saddled," he told Ellie. "Get a lantern and let's go."

Ellie's smile nearly split her face. She took off running to hunt up the light and returned a minute later with two beat-up lanterns. She gave one to Aunt Rose. "Here's an extra light. Just make sure you don't—"

"—leave the lantern burning by itself," Jem finished. A barn and a lantern were not a good mix. It was one rule Jem and Ellie never forgot. The thought of their barn catching fire made Jem shiver, even in the heat.

Aunt Rose set her face in an expression that told Jem she already knew the dangers of an unattended lantern. "Hurry along with you," she said, shooing them toward the barn door. "The sooner you leave, the sooner you'll be back with the doctor."

A new voice suddenly spoke up. "I agree."

When Jem glanced behind his shoulder, Rafe was giving him a half-smile. "Fetch that doctor, boy, ya hear?"

Relief at seeing Rafe conscious and in his right mind washed over Jem. He nodded. "We'll be back in a jiffy." He raced out of the barn.

## CHAPTER 4

# Trouble

J em jammed his foot in the stirrup and clambered into the saddle. He came down hard on his horse, and Copper shook his mane in protest. Jem was tempted to dig his heels into Copper's sides and take off without Ellie. It would be so much easier, and he could avoid her probing questions.

"Don't even think about it!" Ellie said.

It wasn't the first time his sister had guessed what he was thinking, and it probably wouldn't be the last. Jem sighed. His moment for escape had passed. He reached out a hand to help Ellie up. "Better hold on tight," he growled. "I'm not sharing the saddle tonight. And don't ask any silly questions about what I was doing this afternoon, ya hear?"

"Then you better get rid of *these*," Ellie shot back. She didn't take Jem's hand. Instead, she wiggled Rafe's holster, which hung down behind the saddle.

Before Jem could reply, Nathan ran out of the barn, waving a slip of paper in the air. "Mother wants you to pick up a few potions she's low on. She might need them to tend the hurt fella."

"I'll trade ya," Jem said. He took the paper and indicated the extra baggage on Copper. "Take these and hide them, at least for now." His voice dropped to a whisper. "Injured or not, I don't think we should let a perfect stranger have a couple of pistols."

Nathan swallowed. "If Mother sees these, she'll have a fit. Best not to worry her. I'll hide 'em good. You can count on it."

"Thanks," Jem said.

The kerosene lantern rattled and clinked as Ellie settled herself on Copper's rump, just behind the saddle. Jem unfolded his aunt's note and squinted at the penciled words while he waited for his sister. He could barely read the writing in the growing darkness. It looked like she'd scribbled her list in a hurry.

Ellie clutched one of Jem's suspenders with her free hand. "Don't waste time trying to read it. The druggist will know what it says."

Jem stuffed the list in his shirt pocket and told Copper to get going. Ellie let out a happy squeal as they flew down the short drive and onto the road that led to town.

In spite of the setting sun, the evening stayed warm. If it weren't for the seriousness of the situation, Jem would have really enjoyed himself. Copper knew the way to town so well that Jem didn't worry when the night turned the road into a dark ribbon that blended into the surrounding countryside.

A few minutes later, a bright August moon rose over mountains. "Betcha we don't need that lantern on the way back," Jem told Ellie with a grin. "The moon will light our way better than ten lanterns."

Ellie didn't say anything, but Jem felt her laughter bubbling up behind him. Then it hit him. *The moon was full just a few days ago.* "Roasted rattlesnakes, Ellie! You knew we wouldn't need a lantern. You just wanted to come along, so you used any excuse."

"You never know," Ellie said. "Maybe the moon wouldn't

have come up for another hour. You *might* have needed the light. Besides, what if there's a rainstorm and the moon goes behind a cloud?"

Jem looked up. There wasn't a cloud in the sky. "You're crazier than a loon if you think it'll rain tonight." But he was laughing now, glad that Ellie had joined him after all. Two miles was not far on a loping horse, but the time went by faster with someone to talk to. It also kept Jem's mind off the guilt he still harbored over shooting Rafe. "I hope Doc Martin's home," he said.

"Me too," Ellie said softly. Then she gulped. "If he's not, do you think Auntie will take the bullet out herself?"

Jem had given up trying to figure out what their city-bred, eastern aunt would do. On the one hand, she was forever trying to keep Jem, Nathan, and Ellie on a short leash. She'd nearly had a case of the vapors when they'd left the ranch right after chores one day last week and hadn't returned until suppertime. She'd scolded them, but Pa had merely laughed.

The four gold nuggets they'd brought home had not taken away Aunt Rose's worry that the children might have come to harm.

On the other hand, Aunt Rose had settled right down to business when Rafe needed help. She'd mopped up his blood without batting an eye. Jem shook his head. "I have no idea what she'll do if Doc Martin can't—"

Ellie yelped when Copper suddenly stumbled and shied to the left. Jem heard rather than saw the lantern hit the ground behind them. It clanked, and broken glass tinkled, but Jem didn't care about an old lantern. Not when he was trying to bring Copper under control. Ellie had both arms wrapped tightly around Jem's waist.

Jem did his best to keep his seat, thankful he had a saddle to help him stay on the horse. He reached out and patted Copper's neck. "Easy, boy. It's all right."

Copper stumbled again, then shook his mane and settled down at the soothing words.

Jem brought him to a halt. "Let's find out what's wrong." He quickly dismounted.

Ellie dropped to the ground beside him. "What spooked him?"

"I don't think anything spooked him." Jem began to circle the horse. "You know Copper. Nothing spooks him, not even the worst thunderstorm."

"That's so," Ellie agreed.

Jem ran his hand along Copper's rump. He felt his family's rough JE mark—the brand Pa had created from his children's names—then continued down the horse's left back leg. "He's favoring this leg. Maybe he picked up a stone."

It took only seconds to discover the truth.

Jem dropped Copper's hind foot and let out a long, disgusted breath. "He lost a shoe." Horse shoes cost money— money the Coulter family had little of. He glanced back the way they'd come and shook his head. "It's too dark to look for it now."

A little way down the road toward town, through the pine and oak trees, the lights of Goldtown twinkled a warm yellow. They were almost there, and a good thing too. They couldn't ride Copper with a missing shoe. "Let's worry about it later. We still need to find Doc Martin. C'mon." He took hold of Copper's reins and began jogging the final few hundred yards to town. Ellie easily kept up.

Turning the corner onto Main Street, Jem noticed that Goldtown had sprung to life with a bang this evening. The streets were busy most days, but the miners really kicked up their heels on Saturday nights. Wild, rowdy laughter spilled from the saloons and clashed with the clinking of player pianos. The gambling parlors burst from the seams with miners spending their week's pay from the newly reopened Midas mine.

*Crack!* A gunshot made Jem jump. He hoped No-luck Casey and Dakota were doing the deputy job Pa had hired them for. *When the cat's away, the mice will play.* The words of the old rhyme slipped into Jem's mind, but he shook himself free of it and quickened his pace.

Thank goodness Aunt Rose had never seen Goldtown after dark! She barely found time to join the Ladies' Missionary Society, which met Saturday mornings in the church basement. Jem had not let on how unruly the town was in the evenings, especially on a Saturday night. With Pa gone, Auntie never, *ever* would have let Jem and Ellie venture alone into such a sin-soaked place.

Jem planned to stay far away from the worst of the rabble. He knew the town, and he could watch out for Ellie. After all, he was the man of the family until Pa got back.

Dr. Alan Martin lived on Stuart Street, a few blocks past the Express office. Jem's pounding on the door brought the doctor at a run. "Jem! What brings you to town so late this evening? Is your aunt ill?"

"No, sir. Nothing like that." In a few quick sentences, Jem explained what had happened. "Could you come to the ranch and take the bullet out?"

"Of course. I'll get my bag and saddle my horse. Then I'll ride out with you."

Jem shook his head. "Go on without us. I need to pick up some medicine and see if Mr. Clancy can shoe my horse. We'll be along as quick as we can."

One errand completed, Jem and Ellie hurried along Main Street to the apothecary shop. It sat three doors down from the Gold Pan saloon, from which the worst of the noise was blaring. Of all the saloons in town, the Gold Pan gave Pa the most trouble. It was hardly more than a tent, and the bartender didn't seem to care who tore up the place. By comparison, the Big Strike saloon a block away looked like a high-class, San Francisco restaurant.

The racket from the Gold Pan nearly drowned out the banging of the newly restarted stamp mill. The ore-crushing machine had been too quiet this summer. The familiar clanging sounded almost like music to Jem's ears. It meant the Midas mine was back in business, digging deep and bringing up a new, rich strike of gold ore.

"Why don't we split up?" Ellie suggested. "You take Copper to Mr. Clancy, and I'll wait on the remedies."

The blacksmith shop was clear at the other end of town. Through the dim light, Jem could barely make it out. He shook his head. "I can't leave you to run around Goldtown on your own. Pa would have my hide." He yanked on the reins. "Come on."

Once past the Gold Pan, the noise lessened, and the street became quieter. Jem led Copper to the hitching rail in front of a small drug store. It would be a tight fit. The railing was already crowded with half a dozen horses and burros. Most of their owners were no doubt squeezed inside the Gold Pan.

Jem slapped one scruffy-looking donkey over to make room for Copper. He was rewarded with an irritated *hee-haw*. Jem tied Copper up, pulled the list from his pocket, and stepped up on the wooden sidewalk. He turned the knob on the shop's door. Nothing happened.

Then he saw the CLOSED sign. It hung cockeyed behind one of the door's windowpanes.

"Swell," Jem muttered. "Just great." *What was I thinking? Of course it's closed.*

"Mr. Stevens will open up for us," Ellie said. "Let's go around back."

Before Jem could turn around, Ellie had ducked into the narrow alley next to the apothecary. Jem stuck close to her heels. He wasn't about to let Ellie out of his sight anywhere in Goldtown on a wild Saturday night.

Compared to the rest of the town, the alley was a haven of peace and quiet. Ellie rapped on the shop's back door. Immediately, a slender, pretty girl with long, blond ringlets answered.

"Howdy, Alice," Ellie said. "I know the shop's closed, but Aunt Rose needs medicine. Do you think your pa could fill a couple of bottles? I mean, if it isn't too much trouble?"

"I'm sure he wouldn't mind at all," Alice answered with a friendly smile. "Hello, Jem."

"Howdy." Jem fidgeted with the scrap of paper then thrust it into the girl's hand. "Here's the list. Can Mr. Stevens put it on our account? I didn't bring any cash." He fell silent. No polite small talk came to mind, though he knew he ought to think of something. But he never knew what to say to young ladies. They always made him feel scruffy and awkward.

Alice didn't seem to notice. She glanced at the list and opened the door wider. "Come in. I'll give this to Papa and see what he says."

The druggist's family lived in a trim, modest home. Two rooms below and two rooms over the apothecary gave Jem the feeling that he was inside a rich house. Not nearly as fancy as the Sterling mansion up on the Hill, but very comfortable.

Mrs. Stevens offered Jem and Ellie iced lemonade while they waited for Mr. Stevens to fill their order. Jem tried to refuse. He needed to find Mr. Clancy. Ellie could stay here and chitchat, but not Jem. Not tonight.

"Fiddlesticks!" Mrs. Stevens said. "It's a warm evening and you look thirsty. Sit a spell. The blacksmith isn't going anywhere."

Ellie plopped down on the sofa. Jem silently groaned and took a seat next to her. He was trapped—just like a fly in a glob of honey. Ellie and Alice talked about the upcoming Sunday school picnic while Jem squirmed and wished he were anyplace else. *Girls! How can they sit around and drink lemonade and prattle when a man might be dying back at the ranch?*

"Who do you suppose will win the prize this year for the most Bible verses memorized?" Alice asked.

"Jem won last year," Ellie said. Pride in her brother's victory made her grin from ear to ear. "Betcha he wins this year too. He knows more verses than you can shake a stick at. *Way* more than anybody, even more than Lucas Palmer."

*That's not hard to do,* Jem thought. Luke might be the preacher's son, but his friend would rather read dime novels than learn verses during Sunday school. A dime novel fit perfectly between the pages of Luke's big, black Bible.

Jem ignored Ellie's chatter and studied his boots. He couldn't very well clap a hand over her mouth in front of the Stevens' family. Besides, it always backfired when he tried to shut Ellie up.

"You must have learned over a hundred verses last year, Jem," Alice said, clearly enjoying the visit.

Jem's head snapped up. "Huh? Oh, yeah." He shrugged.

"I reckon." It was actually closer to two hundred, but Alice didn't need to know that. Verses stuck in Jem's head as easy as a tick stuck to his leg. He took a big gulp of lemonade and wondered what was taking the druggist so long to fill their order. It was getting late.

Jem drained his glass and stood up. Let Aunt Rose scold him for being rude, but he'd had a bellyful of this conversation. Ellie and Alice chattered worse than a nest of jays. "Excuse me, Mrs. Stevens, but I really need to take Copper over to Clancy's. Aunt Rose will worry if we're gone too long. May we pick up the remedies on our way back?"

A slight frown creased the woman's forehead. "I'm sorry it's taking Mr. Stevens so long to fill your order. Go along and see the blacksmith, if you must. Ellie can wait here with Alice until you return."

Jem headed for the door, eager to be free. He remembered his manners just as his hand touched the knob. "Thank you, Mrs. Stevens, and good evening. Good evening, Alice." Then he jammed his hat on his head and hurried out the door.

As soon as the door shut behind him, Jem sagged against the building and let out a long, relieved breath. He was never gladder to be outside than right now. He much preferred the noisy laughter and rough voices shattering the evening air than the giggles and chatter from inside the druggist's house.

"I tell you what, Copper," he called to his horse as he rounded the alley corner. "All I want to do is get home and make sure Rafe is—"

Jem paused, confused. The hitching rail was still packed with animals tied up. In the short time Jem had been gone, two more burros had been added, as well as a scruffy palomino. But several of the other horses were gone.

Copper was one of the missing.

# ⊰ CHAPTER 5 ⊱

# Missing, Presumed Stolen

**J**em stood frozen in place for a full minute. He could not make his mind line up with what his eyes were seeing—or rather, *not* seeing. His heart flew to his throat and his breath came in a quick gasp. "*No!*"

Breathing hard, Jem scanned the street. There was plenty of activity going on up and down the boardwalk, but nothing looked out of the ordinary. Copper was not wandering around loose. Jem's gaze returned to the hitching rail. He peered closer. Even by the dim light of the street lamp a block away, he could tell Copper was no longer squeezed in with the rest of the animals.

"Where is he?" Jem's throat tightened until his words came out as a whisper. "What am I going to do?" Then another thought hit him like an ax handle between the eyes. "Pa's rifle!"

Jem's stomach heaved. Good thing he'd missed supper, or it would have come up right then. For a moment he felt he might crumple to the ground. He gripped the hitching rail to steady himself and keep his hands from shaking.

Pa had left his good Henry rifle home when he accompanied his prisoner to Sacramento. "You might find a use for it," he'd told Jem the night before he left. "The stage is too crowded for me to pack it along. My Colt will work fine to keep the prisoner from misbehaving." Then he'd frowned. "But mind you take good care of it. If you use it, clean it and put it back on the rack."

Jem had every intention of keeping the rifle in perfect condition. After all, Pa had paid a whole forty-two dollars for the firearm—a huge sum for the Coulter family. He'd needed a rifle when he started ranching three years ago, and now he needed it to do a proper job as sheriff. Jem planned to clean the Henry and replace it as soon as he helped settle their injured guest. He'd even kept the rifle close by in the scabbard for safekeeping.

Now it was gone.

Jem's mind spun. He didn't want to think about what Pa would say when he came home and saw the empty rack above the fireplace. Or the empty corner in the barn where Copper's saddle usually rested. Or worse . . . the empty spot in the back field where his horse—

A huge sob tore from Jem's throat. He couldn't help it. He leaned over the hitching rail and didn't care who saw him blubbering. Nobody could see, anyway. The sun had set, and the street lamps barely pierced the darkness that hung over the town, in spite of the moon's glow. Pa was away, Jem had shot a man, and now his favorite horse and their only rifle were missing.

"Not missing," Jem said between gulps of air. "Stolen." The thought stabbed his gut, and he raised watery eyes. "Who would steal our horse?" He pushed away from the railing, swiped a shirt sleeve across his face, and clenched his fists. "Everybody in town knows Copper belongs to us. Our brand is in plain sight and . . ."

Jem let the rest of his sentence trail away as he bounded across the street. The sheriff's office stood half a block away

41

on the corner. It was a squat brick building with JAIL painted in black on a sign above the door. He crashed through the door without warning. "Somebody stole my horse!"

Jem's outburst propelled the two men bent over a checkerboard out of their chairs. The board, which had rested across their knees, clattered to the ground. Checkers flew everywhere. Some bounced against the floor; others rolled across the wooden planks and under the potbellied stove in the corner. Overhead, the hanging kerosene lamp swayed back and forth.

Dakota Joe, the taller of the two prospectors-turned-deputies, swore. "Sorry, boy," he said quickly, "but you startled a year's growth outta me."

Jem ignored the apology. He heard worse cussing by walking past any saloon in town. He clutched the miner's arm. "You gotta find the thief, Dakota. Round up a posse. Copper's gone!"

Dakota shook free from Jem's grip and backed up. "Hold your horses, boy. No use tearin' in here like the town's on fire. Why ain't you home?"

There was no time to explain. Jem had not stayed in the apothecary longer than fifteen minutes. If No-luck and Dakota acted right away, they might be able to catch up to the dirty, rotten, low-down—

"Come *on!*" Jem shook with impatience. "You're the deputies while Pa's out of town. Instead of playing checkers, you should be keeping folks' horses safe from thieves. I'm telling you my horse was stolen. Right in front of the apothecary shop. Along with a good saddle and . . . and . . . Pa's rifle."

That got their attention—No-luck Casey's, anyway. He ran a hand over his shiny, balding head and whistled. "Are ya sure, Jem? It's mighty dark. Maybe someone mistook Copper for their own. After all, ya seen one chestnut gelding, ya seen 'em all."

Jem wanted to shake No-luck, and Dakota too. They were not acting like proper deputies at all—playing checkers and drinking coffee instead of patrolling the town. How much was Pa paying the two scruffy miners? *Too much,* Jem decided.

"Nobody could mistake our saddle or rifle for their own. Now, *hurry!*" Fear made Jem's words come out rude and bossy. He gulped. What would Pa say if he heard his son talking this way to a grown-up—even if these particular grown-ups were bungling the job?

No-luck Casey didn't seem to notice Jem's backtalk. He reached for his slouch hat and stuffed a pistol into his waistband. "Simmer down, boy. Let's go take a look." He stepped over the checkerboard, crunched a stray checker under his boot heel, and followed Jem out the door. "Be right back, Dakota. Get them pieces picked up while I'm gone." He grinned.

No-luck lost his smile two minutes later. Jem dragged him to the hitching post outside the Gold Pan and pointed a shaky finger at the line-up of scruffy animals.

"Not a chestnut horse in sight," the deputy admitted, scratching his whiskers. "You sure you tied him up right here?"

What a dumb question! For an instant, Jem wondered if No-luck had been drinking something stronger than coffee this evening. "Yes, sir," he forced out between clenched teeth. "In front of the druggist's. I'm sure of it. Copper's missing a shoe," he added. "He should be easy to track."

No-luck laughed. "You loco? It's too dark to track anything tonight."

"But the moon's up," Jem argued. "If you wait 'til morning, it might be too late." This was getting worse and worse. "I'll track him myself," he muttered.

A hand clamped down on Jem's shoulder. "No, you won't. Not tonight. You shouldn't be here anyways. What didja do?

Sneak off to see the big doin's in town as soon as the sheriff was outta sight?" He frowned. "When your pa gets back, he'll—"

"No!" No-luck Casey's words hit Jem's gut like a fist. He quickly poured out his story about the wolf, shooting Rafe, and the reason he'd come to town. By the time he finished, tears were stinging his eyes again.

No-luck squeezed Jem's shoulder then released him. "Sorry I jumped on ya, boy. You've had yourself a day, fer sure. Now, go home and see to that hurt fella. Dakota and me'll look into Copper's disappearance." He chuckled softly in the dark. "Sheriff can't get along without his Henry, that's for sure. We'll do what we can to get your gear back."

Hollow words. By now, the thief was probably miles away, halfway to Mariposa. But it wouldn't do any good to snap at the deputy again. *What did I expect?* With a name like No-luck—who had no luck finding gold—how could Jem believe the miner could find a *horse?*

Jem shrugged and kicked at the dust. He knew if he didn't agree to go home, No-luck Casey would probably drag him there. "I reckon you're right." He felt drained. "Pa's gonna skin me alive."

"Don't go borrowin' trouble," No-luck said. "Sheriff won't be back for at least a week, maybe two. Plenty o' time to hunt down a missing horse." He slapped Jem on the back. "G'night, Jem."

Jem shuffled past the hitching rail and around to the back of the apothecary to find Ellie. His heart was too full of his tragic loss to say much when his sister came barreling out of the druggist's house clutching a brown package tied up with string. It was late, so he just tipped his hat to Mrs. Stevens and muttered a polite "thank you" before turning away.

Ellie ambled along at Jem's side for a block then stopped

short. She gave him a puzzled look. "We're going the wrong way." She had to yell to make herself heard over the racket coming from the saloons on both sides of the street. "The blacksmith's clear over by—"

Jem cut her off. "We're going home."

Ellie's hazel eyes narrowed, and she gripped the package tighter. "Huh? You mean we're *walking* home?"

"That's right." Jem started off again.

Ellie ran up and grabbed his suspender. "Didn't Mr. Clancy have time to shoe Copper? Can't we wait for him?"

Jem hesitated. He often kept things from Ellie, but he never lied to her. Little sisters were a bother, for sure, but he liked being the big brother. Ellie looked up to him and trusted him. Jem wanted to keep it that way.

But he also wanted to spare Ellie bad news if he could. Maybe she'd be satisfied with a simple answer. "No, Mr. Clancy wasn't able to shoe Copper tonight." That was true enough, even if it wasn't the whole story.

Ellie's next words told Jem it was going to be a long walk home. "Why not?" She wrinkled her eyebrows. "Even if Mr. Clancy had to keep Copper overnight, he'd loan us a horse so we didn't have to walk home."

Jem didn't answer. His sister was quick—"quick as a steel trap," the schoolmarm sometimes said. It got her into all kinds of trouble. Like right now. If Jem didn't tell her everything, she'd pester him until he did. Then she'd cry and carry on something awful about Copper being stolen.

Jem sighed. Then he reached out and gave one of Ellie's short, auburn braids a friendly yank. "You ask too many questions." He forced himself to smile. "Copper's missing, but Dakota and No-luck are looking into it. By morning the deputies will be hot on the trail. They'll find Copper and bring him home. But for now, we have to—"

Jem got no further.

"You mean somebody took Copper? Stole him? Right from the hitching rail?"

Jem nodded.

"Dirty, sneakin' *weasel!*" Ellie's howls rose above the clamor in town. "I want Pa!"

So did Jem. Right now. He clapped his hands over his ears. "Hang it all, Ellie. Stop that screeching."

Like Jem expected, Ellie paid him no mind. She turned tail and shot off down the street like a ground squirrel heading for its hole. Jem took out after her. He caught up just as she turned the corner out of town. The streetlamps did not burn on this road, but a bright, gibbous moon lit the way just as well.

By now, Ellie was stumbling along, holding the brown package and sobbing. "What'll we do without Copper? You gotta get him back, Jem. You just gotta."

"I will, Ellie," Jem said. "But not tonight. Tomorrow I'll go back to town and ask around. Maybe somebody saw Copper being led away. He's got that missing shoe; he won't be too hard to track."

But Jem knew this was wishful thinking. By tomorrow, the trail would be colder than dead ashes.

## ⊰ CHAPTER 6 ⊱

# A Long Walk Home

The route from town to the ranch never felt so long—or terrifying—as it did that night. The moon lit up the winding road, causing black shadows to leap out at every turn. A sudden breeze rustled the oak leaves; Jem's heart raced.

Taking a deep breath, he pushed aside the night noises and kept his eyes on the ground. Copper's shoe and the remains of the lantern had to be close by. Finding the horseshoe would save Pa money when it came time to get Copper shod.

A lump came unbidden to Jem's throat. *Oh, God! Where is Copper? Who took him? Please help me find him.* He kicked himself mentally for sitting around drinking lemonade when his horse was being stolen right out from under his nose. *If only I'd—*

Nearby, a howl ripped the night air and echoed between the rolling hills on both sides of the road. Jem's heart nearly stopped. *Run!* His feet wanted to take off, but there was no place to go. He stood still and clutched Ellie's hand to keep her from bolting.

Ellie squeezed Jem's hand until it hurt. She didn't say anything, but Jem knew what she was thinking.

"It's a long ways off," he assured her, mostly to convince himself. The piercing howl seemed to come from everywhere at once. For all he knew, a wolf could be lying in wait just beyond the next bend. The wolf had gone after a calf. Would it go after a boy? Or a little girl?

*Stop it!* He slammed his thoughts down hard and listened for another cry. When none came, Jem quickened his pace, the horseshoe and lantern forgotten. He wanted to get back to the ranch before he heard any more blood-chilling howls like that.

A few minutes later, a coyote began to yip. Ellie gave a frightened squeal.

To Jem, the yip sounded almost friendly. Coyotes were nothing compared to a wolf. "You're not scared of a silly ol' coyote, are you?" he teased. "Didn't you grab the broom and go after one just the other day?" He forced a chuckle from his tight throat. Ellie had been so angry at seeing a coyote sneak by Nugget's usual watchfulness that she'd taken matters into her own hands. The coyote had not been back.

Ellie didn't answer. She hadn't said a word since begging Jem to find Copper, probably because she couldn't talk and cry and walk all at the same time. When the moonlight hit her face, Jem saw her flushed cheeks and red, puffy eyes. Copper's disappearance had hit her hard.

*Good thing she doesn't know about the dead calf.* Jem kicked a rock and clutched Ellie's hand tighter. What a terrible time for Pa to be away! Jem suddenly realized that being the man of the family—even for two short weeks—was a lot more responsibility than he figured. *And I've already made a mess of it.* He kicked another rock.

Rounding the last bend before the Coulter ranch, Jem heard the *clop, clop, clop* of hooves approaching. He pulled Ellie to the side of the road and waited for the horse to reach them. "Is Rafe all right?" he called out.

Doc Martin pulled up beside Jem and raised his lantern. A yellow glow lit up his round, whiskery face. "He lost a lot of blood, but he's got plenty of grit for his size. He'll be fine in a day or two."

He motioned at the package in Ellie's hands. "I gave the young fella a dose of laudanum, but Miz Rose is waitin' on those potions you got." He frowned. "Why are you walking home in the dark? Didn't Clancy shoe your horse?"

"Long story," Jem said. He was too tired to explain. "How much do I owe you?" He forced the question out. After all, he had shot the poor fellow. It was only right he should dig into his gold pouch and pay the doctor's fee. But it hurt. Panning for gold was hard work. It would be mighty hard to part with even one precious nugget, no matter how small.

Doc Martin shook his head. "No need, Jem. The young fella paid me."

"He did?" Except for the pistols Rafe had been packing, he looked like a penniless drifter to Jem.

The doctor chuckled. "He dug out a pouch of coins and fished around for my fee. Miz Rose tried to stop him, but he insisted." Doc Martin lowered his lantern and gripped the reins with his free hand. "You two hurry home." Then he was gone, clip-clopping down the dusty road at a quick trot.

Jem clung to the one good piece of news he'd heard this entire evening: the doctor had been paid; Jem's small stash of gold was safe. He hurried the last few hundred yards home and saw a light shining from the barn. When he went inside, he found Aunt Rose sitting on an overturned pail next to Rafe, who looked asleep.

"You've returned safely." She sighed. "Thank the Lord. And you brought my remedies." She took the package from Ellie and began untying the string. "It's late, Jeremiah. Put up the horse, then you and Ellianna go indoors and get to bed. I'll finish up here."

Jem opened his mouth to protest, but Aunt Rose frowned. "This young man does not need to be watched. He's sleeping soundly." She bored her gaze into Jem. "Not a word. You're not staying out here tonight. Now, do as I ask."

Jem suddenly felt bone-tired. His protest drained away. Would Auntie notice if Copper's tack did not get put away? Probably not. She seemed intent on nursing her patient. "Yes, ma'am," he mumbled.

Ellie was long gone by the time Jem reached the pump. He splashed cold water on his face and thanked God he didn't have to explain about Copper tonight. Plenty of time for that in the morning. He made his way into the house and up the ladder. His attic loft was roasting—as usual. Nathan lay sprawled across his straw mattress, snoring softly.

Jem pulled off his boots and plopped down on his mattress. He propped his hands behind his head and stared up at the rafters. Moonlight streamed into the attic through an open window, right onto his face. He turned away and tried to blot out the thoughts that stampeded around in his head.

A yawn overtook him, but it was no use. As tired as he was, sleep eluded him. Between the stifling heat and his worries, Jem knew he wouldn't sleep a wink the rest of the night.

Mordecai's shrill crowing roused Jem from a groggy, restless sleep. He sat up and rubbed his eyes. A huge yawn made him stretch. He glanced around. Nathan was gone. Jem rose and looked out the window. The sun had been up for at least an hour.

The rooster crowed again. Jem wished he had a rock to pitch at that bird. Mordecai never limited himself to a dawn awakening. He crowed whenever he felt like it—morning, noon, and evening—boasting that he ruled the roost. Not even Nugget challenged him. Right now he strutted across the yard like the champion of a mighty battle.

Jem wondered if the rooster had gone after Nathan again. If so, there was no doubt who had emerged victorious. Mordecai shook his feathers and stretched his neck for another *cock-a-doodle-do.*

Jem yawned again and hiked his suspenders onto his shoulders. He was grateful Aunt Rose had let him sleep past sunup this morning. It had been close to dawn before he'd finally dozed off. He started down the ladder, wondering briefly if the cow had been milked. He heard Nugget whining in the distance. It was late and—

"Roasted rattlesnakes!" Jem yelled as the events of yesterday dropped into his mind. "Rafe!" He jumped past the last few rungs and hit the floor at a run. Barefoot, he tore across the front room, through the kitchen, and out the back door. The screen door slammed shut behind him. He ignored his aunt's surprised, "Jeremiah!" and ducked into the barn . . .

. . . and stopped short.

Rafe sat propped up against a barrel, which was covered with a saddle blanket to cushion his back. He looked wary as he sipped a cup of steaming coffee and stared at the same motionless figure that had brought Jem to a standstill so quickly.

"Strike!" Jem's voice came out as an astonished squeak. "What are you doing here?"

"I'd like to know that too," Rafe said, setting his coffee cup aside. He leaned his head back against the barrel and pointed his good arm at the old prospector. "How would *you* like to wake up and see that grizzled ol' turkey vulture hanging over you?"

Jem pressed his lips together to keep from smiling. It wasn't a bad description. Strike sat on an overturned bucket— arms crossed and stiff as a fence post—watching Rafe. His trousers, red-flannel shirt, and slouch hat looked as untidy as ever, and his beard and hair had grown to matching lengths. His dark, bushy eyebrows formed a solid line above his deep-set gray eyes. Whatever Strike's reason for being here, he looked mighty serious about it.

Strike shifted his gaze away from Rafe long enough to greet Jem. "Howdy, Jem. Jus' thought I'd drop by and set awhile with this-here fella." He paused. "What with Matt gone an' all."

Jem was too surprised by Strike's presence to reply.

"Your pa asked me to lend a hand while he's gone if you needed it," Strike reminded Jem. He reached down, lifted a tin cup, and took four big gulps. Then he wiped the back of his hand across his mouth. "Looks t' me like ya need it. Came as soon as I heard." He raised his cup at Jem and smacked his lips. "That purty sister of Matt's sure knows how t' make a fine cup o' coffee."

Jem's mouth dropped open. Aunt Rose had made coffee for Strike? Poor Auntie! What a shock it must have been to enter the barn and find Strike "guarding" their helpless guest. *I bet she turned tail and ran straight back to the house.*

He saw the twinkle in Strike's eyes and knew that's exactly what had happened.

"Anything's better than the concoction *you* brew," Jem said when he found his tongue. "Aunt Rose doesn't keep an old sock in her pot to hold the grounds."

Strike slapped his knee and laughed so hard that coffee splashed out of his cup. "That's a fact." Then he flicked his gaze at Buttercup's empty stall. "Oh, and don't worry 'bout the cow. I milked her a bit ago."

Jem gaped at his friend. He had known Strike his entire life, but this was something new. "You can *milk*?"

Strike chuckled. "I'm full o' surprises. Ellie turned the cow out t' pasture, and I sent that cousin o' yours to tie up the dog and feed him. Nugget nearly took a piece outta this fella before I grabbed him."

Jem winced. He would have to give Rafe and Nugget a proper introduction soon.

Strike downed the rest of his coffee and handed the cup to Jem. Then he picked up a tin plate and held it out. "Tell your aunt Rose much obliged for the vittles."

Jem stood, speechless. Auntie had fed Strike too? *Willingly?* Why, Aunt Rose hardly let the old prospector come within a mile of the ranch house. She called him a filthy roughneck with no regard for cleanliness or propriety. She'd nearly swooned last spring, when Pa had tucked a bloodied and broken Strike into Ellie's and Auntie's bed without consulting her.

Lucky for everyone, nobody could keep Strike down for more than a day or two. He'd returned to his gold claim, and Aunt Rose had let out a sigh of relief. Since then, she kept her distance, no matter how many times Pa told her Strike was a decent, honest Christian man and their best friend.

"Cleanliness is next to godliness," Aunt Rose huffed every time the family brought up Strike's name.

Now, Strike sat here in the barn—filthy and unkempt as always—and Auntie had fed him. This morning was certainly full of surprises!

Jem took Strike's plate and cup, along with Rafe's, and left the barn, shaking his head. He'd made it halfway to the house when Ellie came running up behind him. Sweat beaded her forehead.

She swiped a loose strand of hair from her face and said, "Didja see Strike?" Her eyes were round as an owl's. "He hates being under a roof. What's he doing here?"

Jem neared the porch and ruffled Nugget's fur with his free hand. He had expected Ellie to pounce on him, demanding he go after Copper this instant. It looked like

Strike's unannounced visit had distracted her. *I might get to eat breakfast first.* Jem's stomach growled, reminding him that he'd missed supper the night before.

"I reckon he's keeping an eye on us, like Pa asked," Jem finally answered. "Rafe's a stranger. But what I can't figure is how Strike found out about him so fast." Ellie trailed alongside as he climbed the porch steps and entered the kitchen.

Aunt Rose struck quicker than a rattlesnake. "Sit down and eat your breakfast, Jeremiah, before it gets cold." She blew out a breath. "Good gracious, why did that filthy miner have to show up? We're in no danger from young Thomas." She took the tin plates and coffee cups from Jem and dumped them in the sink.

Jem paused halfway to his seat. "*Who?*"

"Thomas Rafael Flynn, the young man you shot. He's coming along nicely and is most grateful for our hospitality." Aunt Rose set a heaping plate of scrambled eggs in front of Jem, along with a side helping of biscuits and gravy and a tall glass of milk. Then she lifted a steaming pot of water from the cook stove and poured it over the dirty dishes in the sink.

She handed Ellie a dish towel.

Jem sat down and glanced at his sister. *Did you know his name?* he mouthed.

Ellie shook her head.

Aunt Rose bent over the sink and began to scrub furiously. Suds flew.

Jem picked up his fork and waited. Auntie looked ready to go on a rant about something. *About last night, I bet.*

"Land sakes, Jeremiah! You've thrown this household into a whirlwind." *Splash!* A plate hit the water. Ellie jumped back. "It was bad enough hearing about the dead calf and you going after a wolf, but to shoot a man"—she sucked in her breath—"and then see that good-for-nothing prospector show up and take over without so much as a by-your-leave, well—"

"Aunt Rose!" Jem let his forkful of eggs drop to his plate.

"What dead calf?" Ellie burst out. She threw her dish-cloth on the counter and rounded on Jem.

Aunt Rose deflated like a leaky balloon. "Oh, dear. I *am* sorry, Jeremiah."

Jem was sorry too. His appetite disappeared. From the horrified look in Ellie's eyes, he knew he had a lot of explaining to do.

## ⇥ CHAPTER 7 ⇤

# More Bad News

Jem was saved from answering Ellie by the sound of his cousin's voice. "Give me a hand, would you?" Nathan stood just outside the screen door, his arms piled high with wood.

Jem leaped up from the table and flung the door open. He took part of Nathan's armload and dumped it in the wood box next to the stove. "Need some help?" he asked, eager to escape Ellie's probing questions. "The box isn't quite full yet."

Nathan gave him a puzzled look. It had taken Jem weeks to teach his cousin how to chop wood and split it the right size to fit in the cook stove. Nathan had caught on at last and taken over the household woodpile so Jem could focus on his firewood route. Jem never offered to help anymore.

Nathan glanced down at Jem's half-eaten breakfast and shook his head. "I split extra yesterday, on account of we can't do it on Sunday. Just a couple more trips to carry it in. Go ahead and finish eating." He slammed through the screen door and pounded down the steps before Jem could catch his breath.

Sunday! Jem had forgotten all about it being Sunday. With everything going on, would Aunt Rose still insist on attending church? *I hope not. I'm dog-tired.* He slumped to his place at the table and picked up his fork.

Ellie slid beside him on the bench seat. "What dead calf?" she demanded.

Jem crammed a forkful of eggs in his mouth to give him time to think. He didn't know how to soften his words like Pa could do. He chewed as slowly as he dared, but his plate would soon be empty. *No use putting it off,* he decided.

He swallowed and gave up trying to get around bad news. "A wolf got Pepper. I'm sorry, Ellie, I really am. I was waiting for Pa to come home so he could tell you."

Ellie's eyes swam with tears. "Didja shoot that dratted ol' wolf?" She clenched her fists. "*Did* you?"

Jem winced. "No. I shot Rafe instead."

"So, it's still out there?" Ellie found a napkin and wiped her eyes. When Jem nodded, she stood up. "Well, what are you waiting for? Go out there and get it before it kills another calf."

Jem wanted to. Badly. But he couldn't. Not without the rifle. He pushed away from the table and picked up his dishes. His stomach turned over. He couldn't eat the last few bites of his breakfast.

"What do you want me to do first?" he snapped at Ellie. "Find Copper? Or shoot the wolf? Oh, wait. I can't. On account of *the rifle was with Copper.*"

Ellie took a step backward, quiet at last.

Jem glanced toward the sink. Aunt Rose was up to her elbows in soapsuds, scrubbing away, but there was no doubt she'd heard every word. How could she not? Jem had been talking plenty loud.

"Three days," Aunt Rose said, looking up from her task. "Matthew's been away three days and look what's happened. You lost the horse? And the rifle too?" She clucked her tongue and went back to the dishes. "I told you it was your father's job to go after the wolf."

Jem felt a hot flush creep into his cheeks. Shame replaced his anger. "I'm sorry. I—"

"It's not Jem's fault!" Ellie hollered, whirling on their aunt. "It's that sneaky wolf's fault. Jem had to go after it. He did just what Pa would've done. And Jem didn't lose Copper. Somebody stole—"

"Ellie!" Jem gasped. He'd never heard his sister backtalk Aunt Rose before.

Ellie turned red. Then she dissolved into tears and ran out the back door.

Aunt Rose's face looked as red as Ellie's.

"She didn't mean to sass you, Auntie," Jem said. "She's just upset about Pepper and the wolf, and about losing Copper. I'll go find her."

Without waiting for an answer, Jem dropped his dishes on the counter and hurried out the door. He passed Nathan, who was bringing in another armful of wood, then headed straight for the barn. He knew exactly where Ellie would be hiding.

Jem slipped inside the barn, muttering to himself. Sure, Ellie had gone off half-cocked, but if Aunt Rose hadn't spilled the beans about the dead calf, Ellie would still be inside, wiping dishes and chattering like a magpie. It was hard enough for a little girl who loved animals to learn that Copper was gone. Hearing about Pepper's fate was too much to take in. No wonder she'd snapped.

"Ellie?" he called.

"She whizzed by here a minute ago," Rafe said. He pointed to the ladder leading up to the hayloft. "A monkey couldn't have climbed up quicker than she did."

Jem started for the ladder, but Strike reached out and held him back. "Leave her be," he said softly. "She'll come down when she's good an' ready. Right now you'll pro'bly jus' make things worse."

Jem crumpled to the straw next to Rafe and hung his head. *Please, God,* he prayed, *bring Pa home soon. Too many things are going wrong.* The sun was barely up, but being scolded on top of missing a good night's sleep made Jem want to go back to bed. He stifled a yawn.

"What got her all worked up?" Strike asked. "The fact that Copper's missin'? Or the poor, dead critter out on the range?"

Jem lifted his head. "Both." How had Strike learned about Copper and the dead calf? He scowled at Rafe. *Dirty squealer.*

"Don't glare at *me*, boy," Rafe said. "I didn't tell him nothin'." He narrowed his eyes at Strike. "We haven't talked. He's just been eyeing me like a coyote watching a field mouse ever since I opened my eyes."

"I don't need to learn my news from a skinny drifter," Strike growled. He scratched under his chin and settled himself more comfortably on the upside-down bucket. Jem had no idea how long Strike had been sitting like that, but anyone who could squat all day in an icy stream would probably think a bucket seat was pure pleasure.

"I went to town last night," Strike began. "Watson over at the assay office was checking some ore samples I brought in. So I passed the time at the Big Strike, waitin'."

Jem's ears pricked up. Strike must have been doing some secret prospecting these days if he was bringing in samples to test for gold. Eager shivers raced up Jem's spine. He and Strike often prospected together. "Are you planning another trip? Maybe I can go along when Pa gets back?"

Strike nodded. "Sure thing, partner. So long as your pa will let ya outta school. Ain't it startin' up next month?"

Jem sagged. No, Pa would definitely not agree to exchange a couple weeks of school for a trip into the high country with Strike-it-rich Sam. How had the summer flown by so fast?

Strike went back to his story. "I got the assay and"—he let

out a disgusted breath—"there ain't enough gold in my ore to shout about. So I fetched Canary and started back t' my claim on the creek. It was gettin' late, but I had the moon. Figured it'd be a pleasurable hike."

*Get on with it,* Jem wanted to shout. None of this had anything to do with Copper or the dead calf. But he held his tongue. Strike could never be hurried when he told a story. It was pointless even to try.

"Just about the time Canary an' me was turnin' off Main Street, I heard an awful racket." Strike paused and hiked his drooping suspender back in place.

Jem snorted. "The town's in an uproar every Saturday night. What's so awful about that?"

"This wasn't the usual ruckus—yellin', fightin', and suchlike. Dan Doyle was hollerin' loud enough to wake snakes, crazy-mad about somethin'.

"'What's got you so riled up, Dan?' I asked him. Said he'd stepped into the Gold Pan for a drink, and when he came out his horse was gone." He snapped his fingers. "Just like that."

"But that's where Copp—"

"I know," Strike said, nodding. "Too bad the sheriff's out of town. Those two knuckleheads standin' in for him can break up fights and throw drunks behind bars, but they're not much good at takin' the lead with something serious."

Strike had Jem's full attention now. Copper wasn't the only horse stolen last night! Mr. Doyle's bay was a fine animal. Knuckleheads or not, Dakota Joe and No-luck Casey *had* to do something. They couldn't wait for Pa. They had to go after the thieves.

A slight rustling from overhead drew Jem's attention to the loft. Ellie's auburn head poked out over the edge, her gaze fixed on Strike, hanging on every word.

Strike grinned up at her. "Come on down, gal, and I'll end this tale."

Ellie shoved herself away from the edge. Pieces of straw and hay rained down on everyone below. Jem sneezed.

As soon as Ellie settled herself next to Jem, Strike continued. "I went over to the jailhouse with Dan. That's where I heard about your horse, and about the fella you shot, and the wolf and all the rest." He nodded at Rafe. "I wasn't about t' leave a stranger lurkin' 'round your place, injured or not. Not with your pa away. So I hightailed it over here as soon as I finished talkin' to No-luck and Dakota."

"You sat up all night?" Jem asked.

Rafe looked about as dangerous as a housefly, but Jem was grateful that Strike cared so much about their family. It made him feel warm and safe to have the prospector as a friend—like an older uncle to look after them if things got rough.

"Yep," Strike said. "I've spent many a night awake in my life. One more ain't gonna hurt me none. Plenty o' time to rest once this young fella is up and on his way back to where he came from." He took a deep breath. "And the sooner the better."

The open distrust in Strike's voice made Jem cringe. "Aw, Strike, it's not Rafe's fault he got shot. The least we can do is let him rest until he's regained his strength. Doc Martin told me he lost a lot of blood."

Strike grunted. "I know, partner. It's jus' too bad you went off half-cocked like you did. But what's done is done." He stood and stretched his arms high over his head. "I best go have a look-see at my burro. Ol' Canary ain't used to sharing grazin' space with high-class horses like yours." He grinned.

Ellie giggled. "I'll go with you, Strike."

The mention of the Coulters' two remaining horses made Jem grit his teeth in anger at Copper's theft. "So, did Dakota and No-luck go after the stolen horses?" he asked. "Did they form a posse? I hope Mr. Doyle lit a fire under them."

Strike lost his grin. "Dakota told Dan what I reckon he told you. Too dark to do anything last night."

"But, Strike! Two horses in one night. What if the thieves steal another horse tonight? Or tomorrow night?" A horrible thought suddenly crossed Jem's mind. "Do they know Pa's out of town?"

Strike didn't reply, but the worried look in his eyes told Jem all he needed to know. *When the cat's away, the mice will play . . . No, the mice will steal.*

"Folks are gettin' used to havin' a sheriff around to keep law and order," Strike said. "Your pa's good at his job. But I reckon there's a downside. It's easy to fall back on old ways when he's not around."

"Then find others who can go after—"

"It ain't that easy," Strike said. "No-luck and Dakota are a couple o' green deputies, but your pa left 'em in charge. They'll do what they can."

"The grizzly ol' turkey vulture is right," Rafe broke in. "It takes careful planning to go after a gang of horse-stealing night riders. It's not wise to rush in, 'specially with the sheriff out of town."

Jem whirled. Rafe had been silent during Strike's story. He'd listened with a bored expression on his face the entire time. "It's not *your* horse they took," Jem said. "Your pony's right here, safe and sound. And what do you know about it, anyway?"

"More than you do," Rafe said quietly, leaning his head back against the barrel.

Jem huffed and turned to Strike. "It's not dark anymore. I want to know what's going on. Maybe they found a clue. Tracks. Anything."

"Listen here, Jem," Strike said. "Let 'em do their job. Don't go pestering 'em like a whiny schoolgirl, ya hear?"

Jem grunted. He heard just fine. He wouldn't pester

No-luck Casey or Dakota Joe. He would just go into town and ask, that's all. If the deputies refused to tell him, then he'd figure it out for himself. After all, he was the man of the family now. It was his duty to find out what had happened . . . and to make sure it didn't happen again.

## ⇥ CHAPTER 8 ⇤

# Sunday Morning

Jem turned and stalked out of the barn. No one followed him, not even Ellie. A tiny sliver of guilt pricked his conscience, but he yanked it out and kept walking across the yard. "I promised Ellie I'd get Copper back," he said aloud, "and that's what I'm going to do."

Jem wished he could take Quicksilver or King into town, but the thought of losing another horse kept him on foot. He quickened his pace, ignoring a rock that dug into his bare foot. A quick trip through the front door and up to the attic to snag his boots, and he'd be on his way.

Jem heard the screen door bang shut just as he ducked around the side of the house.

"Jeremiah Isaiah, where do you think you're going? Come inside and get cleaned up. Then hitch up the wagon. We don't want to be late."

Jem froze in his tracks. Then he slowly returned and faced his aunt. She stood on the back porch, hands on her hips, tapping her foot impatiently. The faded dress she'd worn while doing dishes was gone; she was all slicked up in her Sunday-go-to-meeting clothes. A lacy shawl draped across her shoulders; a hat decorated with a small bouquet of summer flowers was perched on her head.

Behind Aunt Rose, Nathan emerged dressed in his city knickers, white shirt, stockings, and high-topped shoes. His blond hair was slicked down with greasy tonic. He looked as uncomfortable as Jem felt.

"Are we"—Jem licked his dry lips—"going to church?"

Aunt Rose stepped off the porch and headed for the barn. "Of course. It's the Lord's Day. Now, hurry up." She disappeared inside the barn, calling Ellie's name.

Nathan clattered down the steps and joined Jem.

"She's leaving Rafe here and going to Sunday meeting like nothing's happened?" Jem asked, stunned. She couldn't! Not today. Not when he had to find some kind of clue to where the thieves had taken Copper.

"I heard her say that as long as that *filthy roughneck* insists on hanging around the ranch, he might as well make himself useful." Nathan shrugged. "I guess it means she can leave Strike to watch Rafe while we're in town."

Jem groaned. Nothing he said would convince Auntie that this was not a good idea. When she came out of the barn with Ellie in tow, her face was set in an expression Jem knew well. He'd often seen the same look on Pa's face when his mind was made up. The Coulter resolve, Pa called it.

Jem raced into the house before Auntie could scold him for dawdling. He splashed water on his face from the kitchen pump and scurried up to his attic room. Quickly, he pulled on his good shirt and a clean pair of britches, then ran a comb through his unruly, dark hair. He didn't bother to glance in the mirror. He jammed on his boots, snatched up his Bible, and climbed down the ladder.

Aunt Rose turned from where she was braiding Ellie's hair into two stiff plaits. Eyes squeezed shut, his sister was definitely not enjoying Auntie's flying fingers. "I expect you'll pass, Jeremiah. Now, run out and hitch up the wagon."

"But what if somebody steals the horses?"

"Land sakes!" Aunt Rose let out an exasperated breath. "In broad daylight? Tied up in front of the church?" She plopped a straw hat onto Ellie's head. "Don't be silly. Surely the good Lord will watch out for our horses while we're worshiping in His house."

"The Lord sure didn't watch—" Jem clamped his mouth shut before the rest of his unholy outburst escaped.

"What was that?" Aunt Rose asked, scurrying into her bedroom to fetch her handbag and Bible.

"Nothing, Auntie."

With Nathan's help, it took only a few minutes to hitch up King and Quicksilver. Jem led the horses across the yard and remembered—just in time—that the man of the family had better help the ladies into the wagon. He settled Aunt Rose on the high seat, but Ellie climbed into the wagon bed before Jem could give her a boost up.

"Don't you want to ride up here with us?" he asked, taking his seat next to Aunt Rose. "There's room."

Ellie shook her head. "I'll keep Nathan company back here."

She sat in a corner of the wagon bed, with her knees pulled up under her best dress. The straw hat drooped over her forehead. She looked little and lost . . . and grumpy. *I miss Pa* was written all over her face.

Poor Ellie! No doubt Auntie had scolded her for talking back earlier. Jem caught her eye and winked. "Cheer up. Pa will be home soon."

Ellie ducked her head, but a tiny smile replaced her frown.

Jem released the brake and chirruped to the horses.

Perking up Ellie made his own grouchy mood fade, at least while they clopped along the two-mile ride into Goldtown. Jem liked nothing better than to drive the horses. The harness jingled as King and Silver tossed their heads and trotted along. Through the lines, Jem felt their delicate mouths waiting for a command.

He glanced up at the August sun. The morning was getting away from them. *Well, Auntie did say she wanted to be on time.* With a flick of his wrists, the horses broke into a faster trot.

"Dear me!" Aunt Rose reached for her hat. Her other hand clutched the seat. Bible and handbag bounced around in her lap. She was helpless to keep them still. "Jeremiah!" she exclaimed.

Jem let the horses trot for two more minutes before he slowed them to a leisurely walk. It took both hands to bring the large animals under control. They snorted and pulled against the lines. *Let us go!* they seemed to be saying.

"Sorry, fellas," Jem said. "Better keep to a walk the rest of the way. I reckon Auntie would rather be late to Sunday meeting than show up with her hat missing and her hair flying every which way."

Aunt Rose did not speak right away. She adjusted her hat, collected her things, and gave Jem a stiff nod. "Behave yourself," she warned. But her eyes twinkled just like Pa's when he wasn't sure about a scolding.

"Yes, ma'am," Jem replied, holding back a laugh.

His laughter and high spirits dissolved the instant they entered Goldtown. When they passed the jailhouse, Jem craned his neck to see any sign of life. *I wonder if Dakota Joe and No-luck are hot on the trail this morning. I have to find out!* The door opened.

The team made the turn onto Fremont Street before Jem could see who stepped out of the sheriff's office. He sighed and pulled up in front of Goldtown's only Protestant church. The tall, white structure—complete with a steeple and brand-new bell—sat next to the schoolhouse. The crumbling, brick school looked pleasantly deserted in the bright sunshine, but it would become Jem's prison soon enough. He made a face and set the brake.

Jem had no sooner tied up the team when the church bell rang out for the first hour. Aunt Rose barely acknowledged his help down from the wagon. She fussed with her skirt, gathered her Bible and handbag, and snatched Ellie's hand. She and Ellie hurried up the steep, wooden steps and disappeared into the sanctuary before the chimes faded away.

"It looks like Auntie made it to Sunday school in the nick of time," Jem remarked, stifling a yawn. "Good thing the horses had itchy feet this morning."

"Mother likes to be on time for services," Nathan said. He crossed his arms and leaned against the wagon, clearly not in any hurry to get to class.

"And for everything else," Jem agreed. He reached up to the wagon seat to grab his Bible. The verses he planned to recite to Mr. Watson, his Sunday school teacher, raced through his head. Not as many as last week, but then . . . *I've been sort of busy, what with Pa leaving and—*

Jem paused just as his hand touched the Book. He glanced behind his shoulder toward Main Street. Last night's calamity washed over him anew. The verses fled. He stared at the quiet street, replaying the events over and over in his tired mind. His eyes closed.

"You all right, Cousin?"

Jem jerked awake at Nathan's question. "What do *you* think? Pa's gone. I shot a man. I lost the horse and the rifle. And"—he yawned—"I'm so tired I can hardly stand up."

"Sorry I asked. Are we going down to Sunday school?"

Until that moment, Jem's answer would have been yes. The church basement was a cool haven on a blistering

August morning. Jem hadn't seen Luke or Dutch or any of his friends since the week before. Sunday school wasn't a bad way to spend an hour. It was the long service that followed—upstairs in the sanctuary cook stove—that made him want to run the other way.

But Jem was in no hurry to join the class now. He and Nathan had been standing next to the hitching rail for a full five minutes. They couldn't tiptoe down the squeaky steps and into the basement without being heard. Mr. Watson would scold them in front of the other fellows for being late. No fun.

*Maybe that's why Aunt Rose wants to be on time for services. Do they scold grown-up ladies if they're late?* The thought made Jem chuckle.

"What's so funny?" Nathan asked.

"Nothing," Jem replied, losing his smile. He slapped King on the rump and made up his mind. No Sunday school today. He would investigate Copper's disappearance instead. "I've got less than an hour before the service begins," he told Nathan. "I can find out if Dakota and No-luck uncovered any clues."

Nathan's eyes grew wide. "You're gonna play hooky from *Sunday school?*"

Jem nodded. It was probably worse than playing hooky from school, and Pa wouldn't like it. Aunt Rose would like it even less. That is, if she found out. "I'll be sitting in a pew next to Aunt Rose before the next bell stops ringing," he promised.

Nathan took a deep breath. "Then I'm coming with you."

## ⚜ CHAPTER 9 ⚜

# Searching for Answers

Jem gave Nathan a puzzled look. "You sure? I mean . . . well . . . you can still make it to Sunday school."

"And let Mr. Watson peer over his spectacles at me like one of his ore samples?" Nathan cleared his throat. "'And where, pray tell, is young Master Coulter this fine morning? Did he not accompany you to Sunday school?'"

Jem laughed. Nathan's imitation of Goldtown's assayer was right on target. For as long as Jem remembered, the proper, East Coast gentleman had run the assay office. He could test an ore sample and evaluate its worth quicker than a hen could lay an egg. And he was never wrong. As a Sunday school teacher, Mr. Watson examined the Scriptures—and his students—just as carefully.

"I'll end up being a squealer or a liar," Nathan said. He shuddered. "No thanks. Besides, I want to find out what happened to Copper."

Jem swallowed his surprise. That was mighty loyal. "Adventure" was not Nathan's middle name. Neither was "risk." Unlike Jem, Nathan did not wake up every morning hoping to hear news of a new gold strike just beyond the next ridge or around the next bend in Cripple Creek.

But over the past four months, Nathan had shown plenty of gumption trying to set aside his greenhorn, Boston ways. He could chop and split firewood almost as well as Jem, and he kept his pockets full of rocks in case Mordecai the rooster came too close. He'd even panned his first good-sized gold nugget last month.

Yes sirree, Jem was ready to admit his cousin had earned his place in gold country as much as any miner. He'd shown real courage during the mine cave-in earlier this summer. *There's nothing like facing death together to make you better friends,* Jem mused.

*Speaking of death . . .* Jem took a step away from the wagon. "It's your funeral, I reckon. Let's go."

"No, Cousin," Nathan said. "It's *our* funeral if Mother finds out."

Jem turned and dog-trotted down Fremont Street. He rounded the corner onto Main, with Nathan right at his heels. The sun fried Jem's hatless head until sweat ran down the back of his neck and under the collar of his Sunday shirt. Both boys were panting by the time they reached the sheriff's office and jailhouse.

Jem did not burst through the door this time. He didn't have to. No-luck Casey sat outside in a straight-back chair, leaning against the wall, with his feet propped up on a barrel. He was busy whittling a chunk of wood into something unrecognizable. Shavings lay scattered on the wooden sidewalk around him. An ancient, single-shot pistol poked out from his waistband.

No-luck squinted up at Jem. "Howdy, boys. Why ain't you in Sunday school?"

Jem ignored the miner's question. "Listen, No-luck. You said you'd go after Copper at first light. Did you find anything? Any tracks? The direction the thieves went? Did Mr. Doyle—"

71

No-luck raised a hand to silence Jem's questions. "Simmer down, boy. One question at a time. I'm worn out this morning and can't take yer yammerin'."

Yammering? He called sincere questions yammering? Jem clenched his fists. "You and Dakota promised to look into it. That's what deputies do."

*Crash!* The chair legs slammed down against the boardwalk. Jem and Nathan jumped back. No-luck rose to his feet, set his whittling aside, and wrapped an arm around each boy's shoulder. "And that's exactly what Dakota and me did," he said softly. "We were up most the night. When we weren't askin' about suspicious characters, we were roundin' up drunks."

Jem said nothing. He didn't want to be accused of yammering again.

"Dakota and me patrolled the streets 'til the sun came up." He yawned and dropped his hands to his sides, then straightened to his full height. "The only horses missin' are yours and Dan's." He scratched his unshaven chin. "The jail's full of drunks, not night riders."

Jem should have thanked him and left. But he couldn't let it go. "Are you gonna round up a posse and go after the night riders?"

No-luck sat down, leaned back in his chair, and picked up his whittling. "Go where? Which direction? At first light, we rode outta town, lookin' for sign. There were plenty o' signs, all right. Horse tracks, wagon tracks, cart tracks, footprints—like always." He shook his head. "The trail's cold. I'm sorry, Jem. I really am."

"That's it? You're giving up? You're gonna let—" A jab from Nathan shut Jem's mouth. Strike's words shouted in his head: *Don't go pestering 'em like a whiny schoolgirl, ya hear?* "I'm sorry," he said. "But surely there's something you can do."

No-luck kept whittling. Shavings flew. "Yep. Until your

pa returns, Dakota and me are gonna patrol the streets from dusk to dawn. No more horse thieves will sneak by us. No sirree."

Jem's gaze flicked to the single-shot pistol in No-luck Casey's waistband. A horse thief could walk right past this bungling miner-turned-deputy. Even if No-luck fired, he couldn't reload fast enough to stop anyone.

"Soon as the sheriff's back, we'll make things hot for those no-good skunks," No-luck said.

"Why can't you make things hot for them right now?"

No-luck let out a breath and paused in his work. "Well . . . mostly we got our hands full keepin' the drunks an' rowdies in line. It's a waste o' time lookin' for those night riders anyway. You know how many canyons and gullies and other hidey holes there are around these parts." He pointed his whittling knife at Jem. "You surely recollect how long Frenchy and his men were able to keep their operation a secret before they were caught."

Jem nodded miserably. There were plenty of places to hide. Highwaymen, claim jumpers, horse thieves, and other gold-camp scoundrels had prospered for years. The miners' court could only do so much. And while the new sheriff had made an impression on the local riff-raff, Jem wasn't foolish enough to believe that all crime in Goldtown had come to a standstill.

But stealing Copper made it personal.

"Dakota and me'll keep our eyes peeled, don't you worry," No-luck promised. "Now, you and yer cousin get outta here. Chasin' down outlaws is our worry, not yours."

*You don't know beans about chasing down outlaws*, Jem wanted to say. But he kept his tone respectful when he told No-luck good-bye. The miner waved them off and went back to his whittling.

"So, what do we do?" Nathan asked when they'd wandered

73

out of No-luck's earshot. "We can't go back to Sunday school *now*."

Jem agreed. Mr. Watson would have a heyday with the latecomers. He glanced at the small clock tower half a block away. It showed another thirty minutes before the church bells began calling the faithful to the service.

If he and Nathan loitered around town in their Sunday best, it might draw attention from any number of folks. Now that Pa was sheriff, Jem—like it or not—found himself at the mercy of tongue-wagging busybodies. After all, a sheriff's boy had to act like a sheriff's boy, not like the rest of Goldtown's young rowdies.

"To play it safe, we better stay with the wagon," Jem said.

With a heavy heart, he thrust his hands in his pockets and headed back the way they'd come. *What do I tell Ellie?* He sighed. *Sisters. What a bother.* Then he kicked a rock off the boardwalk and shook himself free of those thoughts. It wasn't Ellie he didn't want to disappoint. It was Pa.

"Hang it all, Nathan!" he blurted. "What am I going to do?" He didn't expect an answer. Nathan didn't know how to get Copper and the rifle back any more than Jem did.

"Maybe we should ask *him*," Nathan suggested. He pointed to a slim figure plodding along Main Street. The boy was pushing a cart piled high with dirty laundry; his wide, conical hat covered his face. "Wu Shen goes all over town at all hours, picking up and delivering laundry. I bet No-luck or Dakota didn't think to ask the Chinese."

Jem stopped mid-step. Goldtown was home to a good number of Chinese miners. They kept to themselves in the section of town near China Alley and minded their own business. Even so, they were often harassed by the white miners.

Not long ago, Shen's family had lost their diggings up at the old Belle mine. Most had left to work for the railroad, but loyal Shen stayed to help his uncle. The boy was quiet, but his dark, solemn eyes didn't miss much.

"That's a great idea," Jem said. He darted across the street. "Shen!"

Wu Shen paused. When he saw Jem, a smile lit up his golden face. "Greetings, Jem."

"How are you and your uncle getting along?" Jem asked. It would be rude to bombard his friend with questions without even a "good morning."

"Very fine. Uncle Jiang good boss. Say I own part of business one day." He smiled wider. "He like my work."

"Have you heard from your father?" Jem asked.

Shen's hat bobbed when he nodded. "Yes. Father make much money with railroad. He send to China."

Like most Chinese in the gold country, Shen's mother and sisters had stayed behind in a small village in China. The men worked hard and sent their earnings home, but Shen and his father might never see their family again. Jem wondered if Shen missed his mother as much as Jem missed Mama.

"Say, Shen," Jem asked. "Were you pushing your cart around town last night?"

Wu Shen grinned. "Saturday big day for laundry. Everybody need clean shirt for Sunday. Very busy with deliveries, even past moonrise."

Past moonrise? Better and better. "Did you happen to see Copper last night?"

Shen frowned, but Jem went on before he could answer. "Ellie and I came to town last night. Long, horrible story. I tied Copper up by the druggist's, and when I came out he was gone. Stolen. Mr. Doyle's horse was stolen too."

Shen didn't say anything, but his face looked grave. He wrinkled his black brows and stood quietly, his dark gaze looking past Jem's shoulder. Finally, he said, "I do not know.

Maybe. Many horses in Goldtown. I see no one ride horse colored like Copper."

Jem let out the breath he'd been holding; his heart dropped to his toes.

Then a light came on in Shen's eyes. "I return very late to Uncle's. China Alley dark, even with moon. But a rider pass me." He paused.

"And?" Jem prompted. "Was he riding Copper?" *I hope not. Not with his missing shoe.*

Wu Shen shook his head. "No. He ride black horse. But he have chestnut horse with him."

Jem whooped. A clue at last!

## ⊰ CHAPTER 10 ⊱

# A Clue in the Dust

Jem grasped Shen by the shoulders. "You sure?"
"Yes, I remember. Rider call insults at me. Say I block his way."

Jem whirled on Nathan. "I bet the thief was using China Alley to sneak out of town. Hardly anyone ever goes over there. Maybe we can find some tracks."

"If it was even Copper he was leading."

Nathan's remark yanked Jem back to earth. "There's only one way to find out." He turned to Shen. "Will you show us where the rider went? We'll help you push your cart back to Jiang's."

Shen bobbed his head in quick agreement. The boys pushed the laundry cart along Pacific Street then turned onto Stockton. The cart jerked and bumped another half block until China Alley came into view. The boys entered the narrow passageway, which was lined on both sides with small shacks and Chinese shops.

Jem let go of the cart and leaned over the mound of dirty washing to catch his breath. Nathan stood bent over, his hands resting on his knees. "I thought . . ." He swallowed and looked up. "I thought we're supposed to rest on Sunday."

"Later," Jem said, straightening. "The clock's ticking, and we can't be late for church."

Shen abandoned his cart and motioned the boys to follow him. He led them past an herb shop and an open-air market. Live chickens squawked from cages. The odor of charcoal wafted on the breeze. Sunday was not a rest day for the Chinese. A handful of men mingled, conversing in high, singsong voices. A small group of boys playing tag rushed past.

Jem bit his lip. Were there any hoofprints left?

Shen stopped in front of his uncle's laundry, which stood near the far end of the alley. There was less foot traffic here, and Jem's eyes scanned the ground for tracks.

"He go that way," Shen said. He pointed down the alley, past Broad Street and out of town.

Jem nodded his thanks and kept his eyes on the ground. Hoofprints were everywhere. Jem knew very little about tracking, but he could tell more than one horse had passed by. "Copper lost a shoe," he said. "It should be easy to tell the difference from any shod tracks."

Nathan shook his head. "It doesn't look easy to me. All these tracks look alike."

Jem let out a breath. Nathan was right. It wasn't easy at all. The tracks were mixed together, one horse smashing out the prints of another in a confusing muddle. Jem squatted next to three or four prints that looked more distinct. All were shod.

"Here," Shen called. He crouched several yards away.

Jem shot to his feet and ran over to his friend. He looked down. One track stood out. It showed a clear impression of a horse's frog—the middle part of his bare foot. To Jem, it looked beautiful. "It's Copper," he said softly. "Let's see how far we can track him before the prints give out."

He ran two more blocks to the edge of town. The prints

showed clearly. They led in the direction of a little-used road Jem knew ended not far out of town.

"Now?" Nathan shouted. "Those tracks could go on for miles."

"I hope so!" Jem yelled back and kept running. He wanted to find as many prints as possible before they faded away in the rocky, trackless high country of the Sierra Nevada. No-luck and Dakota might be willing to investigate if they knew where to go.

Then again . . . waiting for the sheriff seemed to be their answer for anything they didn't want to do. *Does Pa need to tell them when to buckle their belts too?*

Jem quickly regretted his quick judgment. No-luck and Dakota were decent deputies, so long as the sheriff did the leading. Perhaps Pa should have hired deputies with more gumption, but how could he know Goldtown would be hit the minute he was out of sight? Things had settled down since the Midas mine reopened and the miners had gone back to work.

*"Lousy timing,"* Pa would say. Then he would thank his deputies and pay them anyway.

"If they've got their hands full with the town riff-raff, then I'll have to get our gear back myself," Jem said. He ran a few more steps. "No matter what."

He forgot everything else until Nathan clapped a hand on his shoulder and gasped, "We have to go back. The church bell is gonna ring any minute."

Jem didn't care about the bell. Not since he'd found Copper's tracks.

Nathan yanked him around. "Mother might overlook our skipping Sunday school, but she'll never forgive us if we miss the service." He tightened his grip on Jem's shoulder. "She won't let us leave the ranch until Uncle Matt gets home. Now, come *on.*"

For the last few minutes, a haze had clouded Jem's good

sense. Nathan's words cleared his head. He blinked and looked around. How far from town had they come? Wu Shen was nowhere in sight; Jem could barely make out China Alley.

A wave of panic swept over him. He could not be confined to the boundaries of the ranch—not when he'd finally found a clue. "You're right," he admitted. "We'll have to come back later."

Nathan nodded, and the boys took off toward town.

"Please, God," Jem prayed on the run, "don't let anything wipe those prints out."

Nathan panted to keep up. "And give wings . . . to our feet!"

They were still a block away from church when the bells began to sound. Hot, sweaty, and gasping for breath, Jem pushed his legs into a faster sprint. Dust rose with each clomp of his boots. To his astonishment, Nathan stayed at his side.

The last chime was still sounding when the boys reached the church. Jem slowed his pace to a crawl and climbed the steps as if he had all the time in the world. He hoped his and Nathan's flushed faces didn't give them away.

The sanctuary was hotter than the inside of an oven. Most worshipers were fanning themselves. Red faces showed everywhere.

*Thank you, God!* Jem and Nathan slipped into a pew beside Ellie just as Reverend Palmer asked the congregation to stand for the opening hymn. A small pump organ blared out the introduction to "A Mighty Fortress Is Our God," and Jem sighed his relief.

Aunt Rose hadn't twitched an eyelash at their last-minute arrival.

Jem braced himself for his "funeral" as soon as the horses and wagon left the churchyard. He had watched Mr. Watson, his Sunday school teacher, pull Aunt Rose aside after the service. Jem knew the man was not asking about his aunt's health. *Nathan could have at least ridden up front to share the scolding with me,* he fumed silently.

A minute went by. Then two. No scolding. Instead, Aunt Rose quizzed Jem about Reverend Palmer's message and the text. Jem had tucked away the Scripture verses and one or two main points before dozing off against his will.

When he answered her questions correctly, Aunt Rose nodded. Then she flicked a piece of lint from her skirt. "Mr. Watson occasionally takes too much upon himself. I suggested he wait and bring a certain matter up with Matthew when he returns."

Just like that, it was over. For the second time in two days, Jem felt a surge of gratitude toward his aunt. Driving the horses took both arms, so he couldn't hug her this time, but his heart felt much lighter. "Yes, ma'am," he said meekly.

By the time the horses trotted up the driveway, Aunt Rose had brought the conversation around to her favorite subject—Strike-it-rich Sam. "Why can't he go back to his claim and mind his own business?" she ranted. "Jeremiah, you are perfectly capable of keeping an eye on our helpless young guest. After all, Matthew left the ranch in your care. The gall of that miner to show up in the middle of the night!" She huffed. "I refuse to cook another meal for—"

Jem pulled the horses to a sudden stop in front of the barn.

Aunt Rose yelped her surprise and clung to the wagon seat. She gave Jem a sour look but did not finish her sentence.

Which was just as well. Jem was glad his aunt thought he could watch out for Rafe, but he was mighty tired of her bad-mouthing Strike. Especially when his friend stood right there in the barn's open doorway.

"Howdy," he greeted the returning worshipers.

Aunt Rose let Jem help her to the ground. She gave Strike

a stiff, polite nod then hurried up the porch steps. "Ellianna!" she called. "I need your help laying out dinner."

Ellie groaned, jumped down from the wagon, and followed Aunt Rose into the house.

Strike chuckled. "Rosie don't like me much, does she?"

"Mother's just not used to you yet," Nathan said. "Give her time." He paused. "*I* like you."

"Well, thanks, young fella." He ruffled Nathan's hair. "You ain't such a greenhorn as you first appeared."

Jem grinned. Coming from Strike, that was high praise. There was nothing the prospector despised more than know-it-all city folks showing off their cocky ways in the gold fields. More than likely, they ended up falling into a crevasse or getting lost or hightailing it back to where they came from when they couldn't adapt.

"How's Rafe?" Jem asked.

Strike shrugged. "He's on his feet, frettin' over his pony. Both front legs look pretty stove-up."

Jem dodged around Strike and ducked into the barn. *Thank you, God, for healing him so quickly!* Jem felt as though a huge burden had been lifted from his shoulders. Shooting Rafe had weighed heavily on him.

Rafe was squatting next to his horse in Copper's unused stall. The mustang's legs looked painfully swollen.

"How are you?" Jem asked.

"I'm alive, but Miwok's not happy." He shook his head. "I shouldn't have ridden him so hard. He's put on a lot of miles in his life." Rafe stood. "I could use some help tending him," he said, indicating his arm. It hung in a rough sling.

Jem nodded, eager to help. "We've got plenty of liniment and old rags. Just let me unhitch the horses and eat a quick dinner first. Ellie can boil water for hot packs." He smiled. "Don't worry. Your pony will be right as rain in no time."

Before Rafe could reply, Jem was out the door.

## ⊰ CHAPTER 11 ⊱

# Pony Express Rider

Hot packs on a hot day, dipped in boiling-hot water and wrung out, then wrapped around a horse's forelegs. Over and over again. What a miserable way to spend a Sunday afternoon.

Jem glanced down at his hands. They looked as swollen as the pony's legs and red as fire. They felt like fire too. Rafe was not much help. One-handed, he could do little more than keep the long bandages off the barn floor while Jem wrapped the horse's legs from pastern to elbow.

Ellie squatted nearby, offering advice. An empty teakettle lay on its side next to her. "Are you sure the water's hot enough? You let it cool down too long last time. And you gotta wrap it tighter or else—"

"Roasted rattlesnakes!" Jem burst out. "Don't I have enough trouble without your pestering?" He wadded up a cold, soggy rag and pitched it at her.

*Smack!*

Ellie's muffled squeal told Jem his aim was perfect. She peeled the wad away from her face and pitched it back but missed. It hit Rafe with a *splat*. "Sorry," Ellie murmured and kept quiet after that.

Jem wished Nathan had stayed to help, but his cousin had given up after he'd dipped his hands in the scalding water the first time. He and Strike were no doubt snoozing under a tree somewhere. *I wish I could take a nap*, Jem complained silently. But his desire to "make it up" to Rafe kept him crouched next to a steaming pan of water for two hours.

"That should do it," Rafe finally said. "Miwok's perking up, and the swelling's gone down." He opened a bottle of liniment Jem had found in the tack room. "I'll rub some of this in, and we'll wrap him one more time. By tomorrow morning, he'll be good as new."

Jem sat back and slumped against the wall. His hands throbbed.

"This the first time you've tended a lame horse?" Rafe asked, chuckling.

Jem winced. "By myself, yes. But I've watched Pa do it lots of times."

"I've wrapped Miwok's legs more times in the past few years than I can count," Rafe said. "All that Express riding really took it out of him." He shook his head. "Shoulda known better than to push him too hard," he mumbled and smacked his pony on the neck.

"The Express?" Jem caught his breath. "The *Pony* Express?"

Rafe nodded. "I was a rider back in '60 and '61." He shrugged. "It didn't operate long . . . maybe a year and a half. But we had quite a time." A faraway look came into his eyes.

Ellie's mouth dropped open. She stood up and wandered over. "You're a *real* Pony Express rider? No foolin'?" Her hazel eyes had grown huge, as if President Abraham Lincoln had just walked into the barn.

"No foolin'." Rafe crossed over to his gear, which Nathan had piled in a corner last night. "I kept the pony, but I don't have my *mochila* any longer. It covered my whole saddle and was mighty handy—and not just to carry mail." He opened one of his saddlebags. "Not like these flimsy things."

Rafe rummaged around inside his pack. "But I do have this." He held up a small, black Bible. "Our boss was very religious. He gave each rider—all two hundred of us—one of these."

"That's a lot of riders!" Ellie blurted.

"And a lot of Bibles," Jem added.

Rafe shrugged and handed the book to Jem. "I didn't read it much. I kept it here." He patted his vest pocket. "I figured it might stop a bullet sometime, or maybe even an arrow."

Jem's heart thudded as he opened the Bible. He couldn't speak. Not only had he shot a Pony Express rider—a hero of the West—but he'd mentally accused him of being a low-down drifter sneaking across their land. *Can I get any dumber?*

A piece of paper fell out of the Bible and into Jem's lap. He unfolded it and read, "Wanted: young, skinny, wiry fellows not over eighteen. Must be expert riders, willing to risk death daily. Orphans preferred. Wages $25 per week." He looked up. "Twenty-five dollars a *week?*"

That was more than most folks made in a month.

"Yep, and I earned every penny of it." Rafe took the Bible, slipped the paper back inside, and returned it to his saddle-bag. "I was sixteen and just the skinny sort of rider they were looking for." He shrugged. "An orphan too. They snatched me right up."

Jem waited. Would Rafe say more? There were so many questions Jem wanted to ask. He opened his mouth, then quickly shut it. It was none of his business.

But Rafe surprised Jem. "My father was an army captain, my mother a Miwok Indian. She died when I was small, like most of the Indians around these parts." His eyes flashed. "A fool white man wanted the five-dollar bounty on her scalp."

Ellie let out a cry of alarm, and Jem caught his breath

in horror. He'd heard snatches of talk about such bounties, but he'd never met anyone who had experienced it first-hand. *God, how can people do things like that to other people?* Sure, Goldtown was full of gambling, claim jumping, and other crimes, but the town council didn't pay folks to kill Indians. Not yet, anyway.

And it never would, so long as Pa was sheriff.

"I . . . I'm sorry," Jem said, swallowing his disgust.

"Not your fault," Rafe said, waving the memory away. "My father was a decent sort. I grew up at the fort. But when he was killed in a skirmish, I decided it was time for me to leave.

I was still part Miwok, and I knew the bounty would look mighty tempting to some."

Rafe squatted and began to rub liniment on his pony's forelegs. "I rode the last leg of the route—Carson City to Sacramento. I changed horses every ten miles, but Miwok was always waiting to run that last bit with me. He gave his all every time."

Jem let out a long, envious sigh. Lucky Rafe! Riding like the mad wind across the prairie. Crossing the Sierras with a mail pouch. Everybody cheering when they saw the rider fly through town with letters from the States. "I sure wish *I* could ride with the Pony Express."

Rafe sat back on his heels. "It's not the adventure you think, boy. Mostly, it was long days with a sore backside, being drenched by storms or chased by Indians. Or trying to keep from falling into a ravine in the mountains. Or nearly freezing to death in a snowstorm." He shuddered. "That happened to me once."

Jem hung on every word. He picked up the last of the clean rags and began wrapping Miwok's legs. In his mind's eye, Rafe grew from no-account drifter to larger-than-life hero.

"It's over," Rafe said, shaking his head. "We lost our jobs when they strung the wire back in '61. No need for riders to run their horses into the ground any longer. Not when the telegraph can send a message in seconds."

"I know," Jem said. "I still wish I could have been a rider."

Rafe chuckled. "You and every other boy your age."

"What did you do when you couldn't be a Pony Express rider anymore?" Ellie asked, eyes shining. It looked like Jem wasn't the only Coulter with a serious case of hero-worship.

"Since I knew all this country like the back of my hand, I hired on as a scout: wagon trains, the army, anybody who needed me. I can track most anything, thanks to—"

*"What?"* Jem jumped up, startled. "You can track?" Thoughts whirled in his head like a cyclone: Copper's hoof-prints; the night riders' tracks disappearing into the high country; being able to find out where they'd gone; maybe even—

"Well, sure," Rafe said, breaking into Jem's thoughts. His dark eyes narrowed to slits. "You got something in mind?"

Jem felt dizzy with hope. "I think I found Copper's tracks today."

Ellie opened her mouth to cut in, but Jem waved her into silence. He poured out to Rafe how he'd skipped Sunday school this morning and tracked the unshod prints well out of town. "I don't know how far I can follow them before they disappear," he finished. "I'm not very good at tracking. But you . . ." He let the rest go unsaid and gave Rafe a pleading look.

Rafe plucked a straw from the floor and twirled it between his fingers. He didn't say a word. For a full minute, he stared through the open barn doors, unmoving, barely breathing. He looked like a statue.

*Please, Lord,* Jem prayed, *let him say yes.*

No-luck and Dakota refused to look for night riders without solid evidence of where they'd gone. But if a grown-up like Rafe backed Jem up, maybe they would do more than just wait for the sheriff to get back.

A fly landed on Rafe's cheek. He brushed the pest away and sighed. "I know I shouldn't go along with this, but your horse is missing because you went to town last night on my account. The least I can do is help you get a bead on where the tracks lead."

Jem felt his spirits rise to the clouds. "Thank you, Rafe! I'll saddle—"

"Whoa, boy." Rafe raised his hand. "I can't promise anything. You show me the tracks you found, and I'll show you where they go, but"—he shook his head—"there's no guarantee the tracks belong to *your* horse."

"I know," Jem said. But inside, he knew those unshod prints belonged to Copper. They *had* to. If they didn't? He refused to think about that. "I'll saddle Silver, and we can ride into town before the afternoon gets away from us." Jem frowned. "Unless, of course, you want your own mount. I can saddle King too."

"No, one horse is fine. Neither of us weighs much. Besides, we're not going far. Not with evening coming on. If there's anything to it, we can always pick up the trail again in the morning." Rafe stood and stretched his good arm. "Now, where did you first find those tracks?"

Jem abandoned the pile of rags and liniment and ducked into the tack room. "In China Alley," he called to Rafe. "The tracks went toward one of the dozens of trails that lead up to the high country."

He found Quicksilver's tack—his reins and bridle—and yanked them off the hook. He brushed past Ellie, who had been following on his heels, and headed out of the barn. Rafe joined them. "I don't know for sure," Jem added, "but I think the thief was headed up to Blackwater Canyon."

Rafe's eyebrows shot up. "Why would you think *that*?"

Jem stopped when he got to the fence. "'Cause that place is full of hidey holes and ravines. Narrow side canyons go every which way." He paused. "At least, that's what Strike says. He calls it the canyon of no return on account of all the prospectors that go in but never come out."

"Is that a fact?" Rafe said quietly, rubbing his chin.

"It sure is," Ellie piped up. "Strike says folks can get so turned around in there that they—"

"Strike's full of tales," Jem said, cutting Ellie off. She could rattle off dozens of hair-raising stories Strike told about the gold country. Most ended in tragedy. Jem suspected the tales were a good way to keep the Coulter kids from wandering too far from home.

So far, the stories had worked. Jem knew where Blackwater Canyon was. He'd even seen it a few times. But he'd never ventured into it. The canyon was a good twenty miles away, up in desolate mountain country. Pa and Strike had been there years ago, but most old-time prospectors avoided the place these days. Every once in a while, Jem heard about a tenderfoot miner who headed in that direction and was never heard from again.

It was the perfect place to hide a corral full of stolen horses.

## ⊰ CHAPTER 12 ⊱

# Hot on the Trail

**B**efore Jem could unlatch the pasture gate, he discovered a snag in his plans. Aunt Rose stood on the porch, waving him over. Jem groaned. In his excitement of learning that Rafe could track, he'd forgotten about his aunt. She might not allow him to take off with their injured guest.

Jem dropped Silver's bridle over the railing and headed for the house. By the time he reached the porch, the rest of the family, plus Strike and Rafe, had gathered. It took all of Jem's coaxing to persuade Aunt Rose to listen. He even confessed what he and Nathan had found when they should have been in Sunday school. How else could he prove the tracks were real and not just a wild idea so he could run off to town?

Aunt Rose pressed her lips tightly together. Her cheeks turned red, but she seemed relieved at the news. "That's all you were doing?" she demanded with a frown. "Following tracks? Mr. Watson implied you boys were—" She shook her head. "Never mind."

Jem clenched his jaw. Did she think he and Nathan were peeking into gambling halls and hanging around the saloons? Mr. Watson warned his young charges often enough how sin could sneak up on them in Goldtown. He must have expressed his worst fears to Aunt Rose. *I don't have to be the sheriff's kid to know better than to go near those places.*

Pa would never have stood for Mr. Watson accusing his son and his nephew of such behavior, but poor Aunt Rose! No wonder she asked the Sunday school teacher to bring the matter up later, when Pa returned.

"Yes, ma'am, that's all," Jem quickly assured her. "I promise I'll be back before dark. Rafe too."

"*We'll* be back before dark," Ellie put in. She crossed her arms and scowled at Jem. Her look shouted, *I'm going too!*

Right now, Jem didn't care if half of Goldtown went along. Even Aunt Rose was welcome. He was in a hurry. Who knew how long the tracks would keep? It was August, and rain was scarce. But what if a mountain storm found its way low enough to wash away the prints? He'd never find Copper if that happened.

In the end, help came from an unexpected source.

"Aw, Miz Rose," Strike said, "let 'em go." He waved a careless hand in Rafe's direction. "I've eyed this scrawny scarecrow night and day. Reckon he's not the desperado I feared."

"He's a Pony Express rider," Ellie said. "He's even got a Bible to prove it."

"That a fact?" Strike's dark eyebrows rose to his hairline. He scratched at his whiskers and squinted at Rafe. "You didn't tell me."

"I didn't figure it was any of your business," Rafe said. It was clear the two men didn't care for one another.

Strike gave in first. "Yer right. It's not." He hiked a suspender up on his shoulder and winked at Aunt Rose. "I 'pologize fer buttin' in like I did last night. Jus' wanted to keep an eye on things like I promised Matt. Looks t' me like a one-armed Express-rider-turned-tracker can be trusted in broad daylight for a couple of hours."

Jem's heart raced. *Please agree, Auntie!* he begged silently.

Strike lifted his slouch hat in parting. "Reckon Canary an' me'll head back to the creek. I been missin' my camp-fire." He grinned. "But I'll sure miss your coffee, ma'am."

Aunt Rose didn't return his smile. "Thank you for your concern for our family."

"My pleasure," Strike said, smiling broadly. He headed toward his burro's loud *hee-hawing*. "If ya need me, send one o' the young'uns. I'll come, day or night."

Aunt Rose didn't reply. She watched Strike-it-rich Sam and Canary disappear down the driveway before she turned to Jem. "I've made up my mind."

Jem's heart skipped a beat.

"You may go, all of you. But be back before the sun touches the tops of the hills . . . *or else*." She raised a finger at Rafe. "You too, Mr. Thomas Rafael Flynn. I don't doubt you'll start bleeding again. You come back and get yourself a good night's rest."

Rafe touched the brim of his hat with his good fingers. "Yes, *ma'am*."

"Thank you!" Jem sprinted for the gate.

Nathan whooped and Ellie shrieked her thanks before they scrambled to the pasture to find King. The horses looked raring to go.

Jem didn't take time to saddle their mounts. One-handed, Rafe mounted Quicksilver and took the reins. Jem blinked his surprise then climbed up behind him. *I guess he's feeling pretty good.*

Nathan and Ellie clambered up on King, Pa's big, black gelding, and the two horses loped for the road. What a dif-ference this ride was from last night! Rafe was alert and rode with the ease of much practice. Jem relaxed. *I wonder if he'd tell me a story about the Pony Express if I ask.*

As usual, Ellie beat her brother to the point. "You said you nearly froze to death in a snowstorm once. What happened? How didja make it out alive?" She coaxed King right up beside Quicksilver.

Rafe slowed Silver to a trot. "I'll tell you but"—he scowled—"no more Express stories, ya hear?"

"Sure," Ellie said, but Jem held back a chuckle. If Rafe stayed long enough, there was no way Ellie could keep her promise. She loved stories of any kind.

Rafe grunted, as if he knew this would not be his only story. "I was crossing the summit, heading down to Lake Valley," he said. "It's only two miles, but that grade is narrow—barely ten feet wide—and steep. And it was choked with snow."

A shudder went through him. "It was April, but in the Sierras, spring means nothing. I'd gone a mile or so when the wind came up in a gale. Snow began to fall, and the flakes felt like needles against my face, blinding me. The howling of the wind in those pine trees was truly fearsome."

The August heat suddenly didn't feel so hot to Jem. He shivered, imagining the cold.

"I was lost in that blizzard for nearly a day and a night," Rafe said. "I dismounted but barely moved, for fear I'd plunge over the edge of the trail. Finally, I sat down in a snow bank and fell asleep."

"Oh, no!" Ellie gasped.

Rafe nodded. "I couldn't help it. Then something jumped on my leg. Nearly scared me to death. I looked up and saw a jackrabbit hopping away through the snow." He drew a breath. "If that rabbit hadn't brought me back to my senses, I would've froze right there."

Ellie's eyes had grown wider and wider at the telling. "It was God," she whispered. "He sent that rabbit to wake you up."

"Maybe so," Rafe admitted with a shrug. "But I made sure I stayed awake after that."

"And you made it out of the mountains alive," Ellie breathed in awe.

"Obviously," Rafe said, giving Ellie a lopsided grin.

By the time they reached the edge of town near China Alley, Jem decided that maybe—just maybe—he'd be content being a gold miner, after all, and leave any Pony Express riding to hardier folk. He remembered how cold he'd been, trapped in the old Belle mine. A blizzard sounded much, much worse.

Rafe brought Quicksilver to a stop and pointed to the ground. "These the tracks?"

Jem pulled himself back from cold memories and nodded. "You can see which direction they go." He pointed toward the towering Sierras. "Right up into the high country."

"We'll see," Rafe said. He dropped to the ground and carefully examined the prints. "Looks like one horse and rider, with another horse being led." He scanned the rest of the area then frowned. "Here's another bunch of tracks, coming in from a different direction. More than one horseman. Maybe two or three." He glanced up. "Didn't your prospector friend say another horse went missing the same night?"

"Mr. Doyle's bay," Jem said. He tried to read the tracks like Rafe had, but they all looked alike. How could Rafe sort them out so easily?

Rafe rose, stretched, and remounted. "Let's see where they go. You two"—he called to Nathan and Ellie—"keep your horse from getting ahead and smearing the trail." Without waiting for a response, Rafe nudged Silver into a quick trot.

Stop. Dismount. Look around. Mount. Go a ways. Start over. It didn't take Jem long to discover why Rafe had found jobs as a tracker after the Pony Express. He sure knew his business. When Ellie yawned her boredom an hour later,

Rafe didn't even look up. "You can turn around any time, missy," he said and kept his gaze fixed on the tracks.

They were fainter now and harder to trace. Worse, any sign of Copper's unshod prints had vanished in the rocky trail that seemed to lead nowhere. When Rafe couldn't find prints, he searched for a broken-off piece of manzanita or a scattering of leaves on the ground.

"We're not going to lose them, are we?" Jem asked. As far as he could figure, Rafe was following an invisible trail.

Rafe didn't reply. He walked ahead of Jem, who was leading Silver. Behind Jem, Nathan and Ellie plodded on. Ellie gave another yawn but kept quiet.

A quarter of a mile later, Rafe grunted and pointed. A few shallow impressions caught Jem's eye. Respect for Rafe's tracking skills soared. "I knew it," Jem said. "Blackwater Canyon." They'd come at least five miles, he reckoned. He turned and shaded his eyes against the late-afternoon sun.

"We can go a little farther before heading back," Rafe said in answer to Jem's unspoken question. "The return trip will go fast. It's the tracking that wears on your patience." He gave Ellie a grin.

Another half mile and the trail came to a rough V. Rafe dismounted and examined the ground in every direction. To his right, the path led up in the direction of Blackwater Canyon. The trail to the left headed toward the vast wilderness of Yosemite, although that untouched mountain valley lay far away to the north.

"Which way?" Jem asked when Rafe finally stood up and returned to the horses. "Blackwater Canyon, right?"

Rafe took off his hat, wiped the sweat from his forehead, and plopped his hat back on. "I don't think so." He waved toward the left-hand trail. "More like Eagle Rock or Poverty Gulch."

"There's nothing there," Jem said, letting out a sigh of disappointment. "I'm sure it's Blackwater Canyon."

Rafe scowled. "Who's the scout here, boy? You got your mind set on Blackwater. Did you ever think those night riders might be afraid of that canyon, like everybody else?"

No, Jem had not thought about that. He shrugged. Maybe Rafe was right.

"Regardless," Rafe said as he squeezed in front of Jem and took Silver's reins. "We've come far enough. The sun is sinking fast. We can take up the trail in the morning. You can even stop by the jailhouse and stir up those deputies with your new facts."

*Maybe,* Jem thought. But it was just as likely Dakota and No-luck would brush Jem's news aside. He needed more evidence. Perhaps tomorrow, Rafe would show Jem definite proof of where the night riders were hiding out. *Tomorrow we'll have all day!*

There was just one catch. When Jem raced into the barn the next morning, it was empty.

Rafe was gone.

# ⤙ CHAPTER 13 ⤚

# Betrayal

Gone? Rafe was *gone*? No!

"Rafe!" Jem hollered, hoping to rouse the young man from wherever he'd hidden himself this morning. He dropped the milk pail and scrambled up the loft ladder. Poking his head above the hay-covered floor he called, "You up here, Rafe?"

A slight rustling sparked Jem's hopes, but they were dashed when a ginger-colored cat pounced inches from his nose. He gave the purring cat a quick stroke then dropped back down to the barn floor.

Jem's hopes plunged even lower when he found no sign of Rafe's horse and tack. The man had left—vanished—without even a good-bye. Jem sagged against the empty stall's railing. "I'll never get Copper back without Rafe," he told the ginger cat, who was rubbing its head against his legs.

Four more cats joined in, reminding Jem that his chores couldn't be put off. He retrieved the pail, pulled out a three-legged stool, and milked in a daze. "Why would Rafe just up and *leave*?" he asked the cow.

Buttercup flicked her tail and looked at him. If she knew, she wasn't telling.

Jem felt his chest tighten in anger and disappointment.

"What do I do *now*? Track Copper myself?" He shook his head. "I couldn't keep up when Rafe was trailing. I won't be able to find prints on my own in the middle of nowhere."

*Especially if the tracks lead to Poverty Gulch or Eagle Rock*, he added silently. *I need Rafe!*

Jem aimed a stream of milk at the cats then squeezed the last few drops into his bucket. He hated having to go inside and break this news to Ellie. She'd followed Rafe around all evening yesterday, begging for more Pony-rider stories. He'd finally given in. Ellie had gone to bed with shining eyes and the promise of "just one more" story in the morning.

"Low-down, dirty promise-breaker!" Jem blurted. Then he winced. Rafe had gone out of his way to help track Copper yesterday. *Sorry, God. I don't really mean that. I'm just so surprised.*

He left the barn and nearly collided with Nathan. "Who's a dirty promise-breaker?" his cousin asked cheerfully.

"Rafe," Jem said. He blew out a disgusted breath and kept walking. "He's gone. Vanished."

"He can't be gone," Nathan protested.

"Do you think I'm blind? He's not here."

Nathan followed Jem up the porch steps. "He wouldn't leave without his pistols, would he? I mean . . . he wouldn't leave for long. Maybe he had an errand or something."

Jem stopped short. There was nothing like common sense to make a fellow feel like a fool. He turned and faced Nathan. "I never thought of that," he admitted with a sheepish grin. "You hid 'em good, right?"

Nathan nodded.

"Wait for me. I'll be right back."

Jem took the milk inside, slammed through the screen door, and rejoined Nathan before Ellie or Aunt Rose could say a word. Then he followed Nathan around to the back of the privy. Aunt Rose had planted climbing roses all over the yard. Here, they grew thick and prickly up the lattices hammered to the sides of the outhouse.

"I wanted to toss 'em down the hole," Nathan said, "but I figured I better hide 'em in the next best place." He carefully reached between the thorny plants and drew out an old gunny sack. "Ouch!" He handed Jem the sack then sucked on a pricked finger.

Jem peeked inside at the two shiny .44 revolvers. "I wonder why Rafe didn't ask for them back."

"You wouldn't think he'd go far without 'em, especially around these parts," Nathan said. "I bet he went to town. Maybe he wanted Doc Martin to check his wound or something."

"Your mother can do that," Jem argued. He rolled the guns up in the sack and stashed them back in the hiding place. But he felt one hundred percent better.

Nathan was right. Rafe wouldn't leave for good without taking his pistols—his *Pony Express* pistols. Yep, Rafe had simply gone to town. He'd be back shortly, and they would pick up the night riders' trail once and for all.

Jem sat hunched on a small boulder, his bare feet dangling in what remained of Cripple Creek. The last three days had crawled by as sluggishly as the narrow ribbon of water trickling past. Rafe had not returned. He was really and truly gone.

"I don't understand it," he complained to Strike. "Why doesn't Rafe come back?"

Strike jiggled his gold pan, but it didn't look like his heart was in it. The stream was running low under the blazing August sun. "Pony rider or not," the miner said, "I never took to him much."

He dumped the contents of his pan and straightened up.

"Maybe he's harmless, but ya can't be too careful. I say, 'good riddance.'" He chuckled. "Ya got yerself a nice set of pistols out of it, I hear."

"I don't *want* a set of pistols!" Jem hollered. Tears stung the inside of his eyelids. The prospects of getting Copper and Pa's rifle back were growing dimmer by the day. "I want—"

"I know what ya want," Strike interrupted. "Yer Pa'll be home in a few days. He'll take over, and then something'll get done. Don't fret yerself overmuch."

*Easy for you to say!* Jem shouted in his head. He slumped lower. Pa was coming home, all right, but *early*, thanks to Goldtown's two useless deputies. They hadn't patrolled the town for night riders like they'd promised. Instead, brawls and gunfights had taken most of their time and energy. The upshot of it all? Three more horses had gone missing.

Stolen! Jem clenched his fists. On their watch!

"I tried to get Dakota and No-luck to do something," he burst out. "Know what they said? 'We're miners, not lawmen. We're too busy holdin' the town together 'til your pa gets back. He'll take care of it.' Then they telegraphed him to come home *right away!*"

Strike squinted at Jem. "And yer not ready for the sheriff's return, is that it? Ya wanna get Copper and the rifle back before he finds out ya lost 'em?"

Jem nodded miserably. "I reckon I'll have to track Copper myself."

Strike cackled. "Yer a sight better off facin' your pa than chasin' invisible tracks into parts unknown." Then he turned serious. "I mean it, Jem. Stick around an' wait for your pa, ya hear?"

Jem heard, but he didn't reply.

Strike squished his way through the creek's muddy bottom near the bank then turned around. "I'm goin' fer coffee. Want some?"

Definitely not.

"No thanks," Jem said aloud. "I better get home." Sighing, he left his boulder and the dirty stream. The two hours he'd spent with his prospector friend had not cheered Jem at all. Strike had no easy answers to Jem's troubles, and now the ranch chores were calling his name.

He scowled and struggled into his boots.

"Stop by tomorrow," Strike offered. He poured himself a cup of coffee and gave Jem a worried look. "We can talk."

"Maybe," Jem said, making no promise. He mounted Quicksilver and touched his heels to the gray's sides. He was in no hurry to get back to the ranch, so he kept his horse at a slow trot. When he passed through town, it took all his resolve not to stop by the jailhouse and "pester"—as Strike called it—Dakota and No-luck.

It would do no good, anyway. Pa was most likely on his way home by now. He wouldn't be overjoyed at having to dump his prisoner off without a by-your-leave and catch the next stagecoach back to gold country.

*And when he learns he has no rifle to do his job, he'll—*

Jem shoved that dreadful thought clean away from his mind without finishing it. But his heart was still racing by the time he trotted into the yard. He saw Nathan on the back porch, peeling away at a large limb with his pocketknife. Ellie was romping with Nugget. Neither looked up at Jem's return.

He dismounted and led Silver to the back pasture. A speck of movement in the distance caught Jem's gaze as he slapped his horse into the field. He shaded his eyes and looked harder. It was a horse and rider, coming in fast from the range. What now? He hoped it wasn't another stranger.

It wasn't. To his shock and joy, Rafe galloped up and yanked his pony to a stop in front of Jem. "Howdy, boy. Miss me?" He grinned.

"Rafe!" Ellie shrieked and abandoned Nugget. Nathan

threw his whittling project down and raced over. Even Nugget seemed happy to see the young man. He yipped and jumped up to lick their recent guest, who was clearly no longer a stranger.

Aunt Rose stepped outside. "What's all the commotion?" Then she wiped her hands on her apron and hurried down the porch steps. "Land sakes, young man, you look good as new." She was smiling broadly. And no wonder. Rafe sat on Miwok's back, tall and straight. No sign that he had ever been injured showed anywhere.

"I want to apologize for leaving so suddenly," Rafe said. "I had some urgent business to take care of and needed an early start." He shrugged. "You knew I'd be back though."

"No, I didn't," Jem said, scowling.

Rafe patted a rifle scabbard buckled to his saddle. "Rifles are fine on a hunt, but I would never leave my pistols. They come in mighty handy. Easier to tote around than a rifle too." He sobered. "But I needed a rifle for what I had in mind."

Jem frowned. What was Rafe talking about?

"I decided that pesky wolf was behind all our troubles. If it wasn't for him, you'd still have your horse." He dismounted and clapped Jem on the shoulder. "Been out to the herd lately? The remains of that dead calf are gone."

Guilt washed over Jem. He hadn't checked on his family's livelihood since finding Pepper last Saturday. He shook his head.

"It means the wolf came back for his meal," Rafe went on. "The trail was pretty fresh, so I went after him. Led me on quite a chase for a couple of days. Then, when I had him in my sights, I missed." He blew out a disgusted breath. "Sly critter, that one."

Rafe circled around behind his horse, where a large, white, feathered *something* fluttered and squawked. "Got somethin' for Ellie. Caught it on my way back. A half-grown turkey chick can't replace a calf, but"—he held it up—"maybe caring for it will help ease the sadness."

Ellie squealed and clapped her hands.

Rafe peeked around the horse's rump at Jem. "Grab the rifle, will ya? You can give me a hand cleaning it. I plan to go after that wolf again first thing in the morning."

"Sure." As Jem reached for the rifle, his hand brushed against the scabbard. An unusual mark caught his attention. He peered closer and sucked in his breath. His world began to spin out of control.

It was Pa's rifle scabbard.

## ⊰ CHAPTER 14 ⊱

# On Their Own

Jem leaned against the horse and took a few deep breaths to steady himself. The dizziness passed. *I must be mistaken,* he reasoned. *This can't be Pa's.*

But he knew it was.

Jem ran his fingers over a crooked C and part of an O that had been gouged into the dark leather near the bottom strap. Except for a few places that showed wear and tear, the scabbard was smooth and nondescript—which is why Jem had wanted to carve their family name into it three years ago.

He'd made it as far as the second letter before Pa caught him and warmed his backside. "If I want letters or any other fancy etchings, I'll take it to the leather smith," he'd told Jem, then warned him to keep away from—

A hand on his shoulder yanked Jem from the past. He spun around, eyes wide and scared.

"Whoa, boy! What's the matter?" Rafe backed up. "Looks like you've seen a ghost. Didn't you hear me?"

Jem shook his head. He felt drops of sweat trickle down his neck. "S-sorry," he stammered, "I was thinking about"— he scrambled to put his muddled thoughts in order— "something else." He swallowed. "What did you say?"

"I said to take the rifle into the barn. We'll clean it later. Then come help Ellie and me settle this little gobbler."

With difficulty, Jem nodded. His stomach felt tied in knots. He couldn't be bothered with a dumb turkey. He needed to sort things out. Why did Rafe have Pa's scabbard?

Jem slid the rifle from its protective leather covering and gripped it to keep his hands still. He didn't want Rafe to see how badly shaken he was. In a daze, he carried the rifle to the barn, set it down on the high workbench, and carefully looked it over. Most Henry rifles looked alike. There was nothing special about this one, but somehow Jem *knew*. It was Pa's.

Reasons for why Rafe had Pa's rifle and scabbard swirled around in Jem's head like a choking dust storm. *Rafe found it . . . no, he bought it . . . no, he borrowed it from . . .*

The only answer that made sense was a dirty one: Rafe was part of the gang of thieving night riders. Red-hot fury exploded through Jem, wiping out any other explanation. He fingered the rifle. He wanted nothing more than to point it at Rafe and haul him to the jailhouse. "But not before he tells me where Copper is," he muttered.

"What's the holdup, boy?" Rafe called from the yard.

"Be right there!" Jem hollered back. He chewed on his lip, deep in thought. There had to be a better way to get answers. Confronting Rafe with the business end of a Henry rifle might work. Then again . . . if Rafe was part of the outlaw gang, it could be dangerous to let on what Jem knew. He had Aunt Rose, Nathan, and Ellie to think about.

"Don't go off half-cocked," Jem warned himself. "Simmer down. Think it through." He paused. "For now, I'll go on like nothing's happened. I know Rafe didn't pick up Pa's rifle and scabbard in town. He must have gotten it wherever the thieves are holed up, which means—"

Jem caught his breath. It suddenly occurred to him that Rafe might not have been entirely honest when he took them tracking the other day. The tracks Jem and Nathan had found pointed straight toward Blackwater Canyon. It was only when the prints became faint and far between that Rafe suggested they might lead in a different direction.

"Maybe he wants us to think the night riders headed for Poverty Gulch, when they're really hiding in Blackwater Canyon." The thought made Jem feel prickly all over. He left the barn at a run and caught up to his family and Rafe near the woodshed.

Ellie had her arms full of the struggling, half-grown gobbler. For the first time since Rafe returned, Jem looked at it. *Really* looked at it. "It's pure white!"

"Albino," Rafe said. "Very rare. Very sacred."

Jem wrinkled his eyebrows. "In what way?" Any turkey was tasty. Maybe an albino turkey tasted better. But holy? Not likely.

"Albinos are considered sacred among many tribes," Rafe said. "All-white animals are powerful 'medicine.' Magical." He shrugged, which told Jem that Rafe didn't go along with such superstitions. "This bird wouldn't have lived much longer with a damaged wing. White doesn't blend in too well. Coyote bait for sure."

Ellie squeezed the turkey tighter. "Never! I'll take care of Snow White."

Jem groaned. What a dumb name! "Where will you keep it? It's too big for the henhouse."

"In the woodshed for now," Ellie told him. "You gotta clear a spot, Jem. Pa can make a pen later."

Pa had no more time to make a pen for a pet gobbler

than he had to pan for gold. "I'll make it," Jem offered with a sigh. "Maybe Rafe can help."

Rafe shook his head. "I got a wolf to track, remember?"

"I remember," Jem said quietly. He opened the woodshed door, deep in thought. *It makes a good story, but I bet you're not really tracking any ol' wolf.*

Rafe headed out the next day at first light. He'd only come by to drop off the turkey, he explained, and to let Jem know the herd was safe. "Thanks for cleaning my rifle," he said. "And . . . I'd like my pistols. Didn't want to bother you folks when I took off the other day, but I feel kinda undressed without 'em."

Jem bristled. He wished Nathan had dropped those guns down the privy hole. Too late now. He looked at his cousin, who shrugged and hurried toward the outhouse.

Rafe mumbled his thanks when Nathan returned. He buckled the holster around his hips and tightened the rifle scabbard to his saddle. "When I get that wolf, I'll be back."

*Sure you will, you lying thief,* Jem fumed, scowling.

"You got a burr under your saddle, boy?" Rafe asked. "Sorry I can't stay, but building a pen isn't that much work. You don't need me."

Jem didn't answer. Let Rafe think what he liked. A pen for Ellie's turkey was at the very bottom of Jem's chore list. Snow White would have to stay imprisoned in the woodshed for a few more days. He had more important plans.

As soon as Rafe disappeared toward the rangeland, Jem drew Nathan aside. "I have to talk to you. Alone."

Nathan's eyebrows shot up. He lowered his voice to match Jem's. "What about?"

Jem flicked his gaze toward Ellie and Aunt Rose to make sure they were out of earshot. Ellie had brought Snow White out of the shed and set her on the ground. A length of twine was tied around the turkey's neck. Ellie gripped the other end. Aunt Rose had squatted and was looking over the wing she and Ellie had splinted yesterday afternoon.

*Dumb bird.* He turned back to Nathan. "Rafe has Pa's rifle."

Nathan's gasp brought Aunt Rose and Ellie around. "What's the matter?" Ellie asked.

Jem elbowed Nathan. "Nothin'." He plucked his cousin's shirt sleeve and led him to a giant oak tree near the barn. The boys scurried up the wobbly slats nailed to the trunk and hauled themselves onto a rough, wooden platform. Plenty of spreading branches hedged them in on all sides.

Jem peeked through the leaves to make sure Ellie hadn't followed them. For once, it was important that she not get wind of what he was up to. She could sniff out almost any plan Jem made, and he usually didn't mind including her. Ellie was quick and smart. She was good to have along in a pinch.

But not this time.

Jem hesitated telling Nathan, but he needed somebody to confide in. His cousin had come a long way from the city kid he'd been at first. He'd grown taller and filled out. He was nearly Jem's size now. A night in a collapsed mine had really helped Nathan lose his fear of the unexpected. *Maybe he'll be game to go along with my idea.*

"Rafe's one of the night riders," Jem said when he'd settled himself on the platform. "Soon as I saw Pa's rifle and scabbard, I knew. He must have gotten them from the gang stealing the horses."

CANYON OF DANGER

Nathan's eyes were round with shock. "Do you suppose he's lying about being an Express rider? I mean, how could a—"

"No." Jem shook his head. "I think he's a real rider, but things change. People change." He slammed a fist into his palm. "He used those Express stories to keep us thinking he's some kind of hero. And I fell for it—hook, line, and sinker." *Just like a dumb fish!*

Nathan sat motionless while Jem laid out his plans. He explained why he thought Rafe and the others were in Blackwater Canyon—how Rafe had most likely tricked them with his tracking skills. He reminded his cousin how unwilling Goldtown's deputies were to investigate where the thieves had gone.

"They're waiting for Pa to take over," Jem finished. He leaned back against a thick limb. "I bet Rafe also knows that Pa is coming home early. He's probably gone to tell 'em it's time to clear out. If only . . ." He let out a long, deep sigh.

Nathan leaned forward. "If only *what?*"

"Dakota and No-luck say they don't have time to nose around, following tracks in every direction. But what if they knew for sure where the thieves are holed up?" Jem pondered. Dakota Joe and No-luck Casey weren't stupid—just inexperienced. "If they could lock those thieves in a jail cell, Pa would be mighty impressed."

"So, you're gonna tell the deputies the night riders are in Blackwater Canyon?" Nathan asked. He broke off a twig and began twirling it between his fingers. "Will they believe you?"

Jem laughed. "Not without proof. That's why I'm gonna get proof. Today."

"Today?" The twig fell from Nathan's fingers. "But . . . but—"

"No buts, Nathan." Jem clasped his arms around his

knees. "It's gotta be soon, before the thieves disappear clear to Nevada. I want to find proof they're up there—proof No-luck will believe. Nothing else. It's a long way, but if we leave right now and ride hard, we can make it to the canyon and back in one day."

"*We?*" Nathan's voice rose to a squeak.

Jem nodded. "We can't tell a soul, especially not Ellie. Silver can carry three most days, but we're going up to the high country. Two on his back is plenty for that. Besides, it's too dangerous for a little girl." He held Nathan's wide-eyed stare and waited.

*Please say you'll come along,* Jem pleaded silently. He didn't want to go alone.

Nathan picked up the twig and twirled it a few more times. Then he gave Jem a slight nod. "I guess it's up to us."

## ⊰ CHAPTER 15 ⊱

# Blackwater Canyon

It was surprisingly easy to leave the ranch.

Nathan bridled Quicksilver while Jem rummaged around for the canteens and filled them at the pump. He found their hats and asked Aunt Rose to pack a gunnysack with sandwiches and a handful of molasses cookies.

"We're going out to the herd," Jem explained when she looked at him suspiciously.

It was the truth. The cattle were Jem's responsibility, and he hadn't checked on them in days. "Then we might do a little tracking," he added. "Rafe's not here, but I learned a lot from him. We'll be gone all day."

Aunt Rose wrinkled her forehead. "You're not going through town, are you?"

"No, ma'am." Town was the last place Jem wanted to visit today.

She relaxed and smiled. "All right then. It appears the wild countryside is safer than Goldtown these days, what with all the rowdiness and thievery going on. Thank the good Lord that Matthew will be home in a day or two."

News of Pa's early return had put Aunt Rose in high

spirits. Jem could think of no other reason why she was so free with her permission this morning. "Is Ellianna going along?" she asked.

Jem grinned. "Not this time."

It was the one good thing that had come from Rafe's return. Jem had expected he'd have to sneak away—or engage in battle with his sister. To his surprise, Ellie had waved away the idea of tagging along. She was fully occupied with the needs of her new pet.

"Maybe it's not such a dumb bird after all," Jem said as he tied the grub sack to his saddle horn. He handed Nathan his hat and canteen then checked the girth. Silver had a bad habit of blowing himself up with air. More than once, a loose saddle had sent Jem tumbling off the horse. He couldn't let that happen today.

Jem cinched the saddle tighter, mounted Silver, and gave Nathan his hand. "Let's get going."

Afraid that Aunt Rose might suddenly put two and two together and come up with the correct sum—where the boys' tracking adventure could lead them—Jem dug his heels into Silver. They were out of the yard and heading toward the distant range before the dust settled.

"I can't figure out why Mother didn't ask more questions," Nathan said. "If she knew where we're really headed, she'd . . ." His voice trailed off.

"She asked if we were going to town," Jem replied. "She knows that's where we tracked Copper before. What I don't think she realizes is that we can cut two or three miles off by starting from the ranch. No need to go all the way to town just to double back. I can find the trail from here."

"Really?" Nathan went silent for a minute. Then, "Maybe that explains why Rafe was crossing our range the other day. You know, when you shot him? He could've been taking a shortcut up to the canyon."

Jem gasped. *Why didn't I think of that?* He pulled back on Silver's reins and brought the horse to a jarring stop.

Nathan clutched Jem's waist. "Give me a little warning, will ya?"

"Sorry." He turned around and stared at his cousin. "I bet you're right about Rafe. It's looking more and more like Blackwater Canyon is the thieves' hiding place." His heart skipped at the thought of going anywhere near that dark, dangerous place. "But we're not going *in*," he reminded himself, gripping the reins. "Giddup, Silver."

The horse leaped into a smooth, swinging lope. Before Jem knew it, the Coulter cattle came into sight. He slowed Silver and took a few minutes to count the cows and calves. Then he counted them again, just to make sure.

". . . twenty-eight, twenty-nine, and there's Samson." He pointed out the new bull grazing nearby. "They're all here. Let's go."

"That was fast," Nathan remarked.

"And a stroke of luck for us," Jem said. "Usually they're scattered all over the place." To get an accurate head count, Jem had prepared himself to go after every straggler hiding in the scrubby brush. He wanted to keep his conscience clear about tending the herd. Rafe had told him the herd was safe, but Jem needed to be sure in his own mind. *Besides, I don't believe Rafe anymore.*

Grateful for the extra time, Jem urged his horse forward. He didn't push him. Every couple of miles he slowed Silver to a jog so he could catch his wind, then nudged him back into a lope. His gait ate up the miles as they rode deeper into the foothills.

The trail soon turned steeper and rougher, and Jem was forced to slow his horse to a hurried walk. Any faster, and Silver might stumble and spill his riders.

Ahead of them, the sun rose high above the rugged

mountain peaks. The path, always climbing, weaved between steep hills covered with pine, fir, and manzanita. Faint animal trails veered off in several directions, cutting across the dark ridges.

"I sure hope you know where you're going," Nathan muttered.

Jem pointed to a jagged, double-peaked formation. "As long as I keep those peaks in sight, I know I'm on the right track. They're hard to miss."

Hours later, Jem stopped near a large, rocky outcropping to rest and water the horse. Alongside the trail, a brook splashed over the rocks in a small waterfall. Silver wasted no time dipping his nose in the water.

Jem unscrewed the top from his canteen and took a long drink. Nathan followed suit, then gasped.

Jem twisted around. Far below and to the west dark, forested hills stretched for miles. *Goldtown and the ranch are down there somewhere,* he told himself. But in the middle of the vast wilderness, Jem suddenly felt as if he and Nathan were the only living souls on earth. He glanced up at the double peaks to make sure he wasn't lost.

"We're up awfully high," Nathan said, capping his canteen. He slung it over his shoulder and slid off Silver. "I need to walk around before I end up glued to the horse."

Jem joined him. It felt good to stretch his legs. Four straight hours on horseback had made him stiff and sore all over. He remembered how long Rafe had to stay in a saddle when he rode for the Express. Eight hours? Ten? Jem groaned. "I'm glad I'm not a Pony rider after all."

"Me too," Nathan said. He loosened the grub sack from the saddle. "Let's eat."

The boys dug into their bread-and-butter sandwiches and cookies. Then they washed it all down with a few swallows from their canteens.

Jem looked up. The sun was just past its highest point. "We've made good time," he remarked. "The ground levels off some after this, until just before we get to the canyon's mouth. I remember that much." He dropped his gaze to the ground. Like he expected, no tracks showed on the hard, rocky trail. He couldn't even find Silver's tracks.

Nathan shaded his eyes and glanced back the way they'd come. Then he looked toward the peaks. "You're *sure* you know where we're going?"

Jem nodded. "I told you, I've been up here and seen the canyon before. I've just never gone in." He mounted Silver and reached for Nathan's hand. "And I don't plan on going in this time, either. I've heard too many stories."

"Why is it called Blackwater Canyon?" Nathan asked. "Is the water really black?"

Jem nudged Silver. "I dunno. I haven't seen it. But Strike says black sand in the creek bottom makes the water look black. Plus, steep rock walls on both sides of the stream fill the whole canyon with shadows." He shivered, glad for the noonday sun overhead.

"I wonder if there's any gold in there," Nathan murmured.

"Probably more gold than you can shake a stick at," Jem said. "But nobody'll ever bring it out." He lowered his voice. "The canyon holds the bones of gold-hungry prospectors too. Strike's one of the few miners who went in and actually found his way out."

Jem was pretty sure the night riders were holed up some-where near the main entrance. They'd be crazy to go deeper into the maze of narrow gorges and ravines that snaked their way through the canyon. Jem hoped to find a good spot to peek down into the canyon and look for signs—maybe smoke from a fire or some kind of movement.

"We'll scout around," Jem told Nathan. "Then back home

as fast as lightning. I hope Rafe hasn't already warned them to clear out." *Please, God! Don't let Copper be gone yet.*

Half an hour later, Jem brought Silver to a halt.

"I don't see a canyon, or any sign of an entrance *to* a canyon," Nathan said when he and Jem slid off the horse. He looked around. "Just trees, rocks, steep hills, and . . . more trees."

Jem tied Silver to a sturdy pine limb. "The entrance is over there quite a ways." He pointed off in the distance, farther along the trail. Then he started for the hill. "If we get too close to the entrance, we're bound to be heard and spotted. So, we're going to climb this hill and look down *into* the canyon."

Nathan seemed to understand the sense of that. He followed Jem through the trees, around boulders the size of the ranch house, and across ledges of slippery shale. "How high does this peak go?" he asked twenty minutes later.

Jem glanced behind his shoulder at his struggling cousin. Nathan was leaning against a giant sugar pine, gasping for breath. Jem didn't feel much better, but he couldn't stop now. He took a quick gulp from his canteen and wiped his mouth. "Not far," he promised. He hoped so, anyway. He'd never seen this hill in his life. *But it must overlook the canyon. Where else could it go?*

When Jem finally reached the top, he leaned over, rested his hands on his knees, and sucked in great gulps of air. Then he straightened and glanced around. Everywhere, pines grew thick as carrots. Through the branches, Jem could see where the world suddenly dropped off. He crept closer and peered over the canyon's rim.

Trees covered the steep slopes, but far below, Jem could make out a thin wisp of smoke. It trailed up into the early afternoon sky. He followed the smoke with his eyes to the canyon floor. On the far side, a crude corral butted up against a steep, rocky cliff. It held what looked to Jem like toy horses. He didn't try to count them. The corral looked full.

Nathan brushed up against Jem, panting. "See anything?"

"Plenty." Jem grinned. "Horses. A campfire. Look."

Nathan followed Jem's pointing finger. "You're right. They're here. Your deputy friends will surely have to do something now."

Jem agreed. He'd seen enough to convince even No-luck and Dakota to take action. No need to stick around any longer. He turned away from the ledge. "Let's go home."

Going down went much faster than climbing up. The boys skidded and dodged trees as they barreled down the hillside slippery with dead grass, old pine needles, and loose stones. Twice, Jem fell head over heels, but he jumped up and kept running. Near the bottom, he paused to catch his breath and his balance. At his feet lay a sugar-pine cone nearly two feet long.

He gave a low whistle. "Ellie will love this," he said, scooping it up. "I've never seen one so—"

"Shhh!" Nathan grabbed Jem's shirt and yanked him behind a tree. He put a finger to his lips.

*What's wrong?* Jem mouthed. He carefully set the pine-cone on the ground.

Nathan pressed his mouth close to Jem's ear. "Somebody's with Silver."

Jem's heart flew to his throat. He peeked around the sugar pine's trunk. *Thank you, God, for Nathan's sharp eyes!* They were still some distance away, but Jem could see two men circling his horse.

Jem jerked around and slid down behind the tree. "This can't be happening," he whispered. First Copper. Now Quicksilver. *Pa will never leave me in charge of anything ever again.*

"Is it the night riders?" Nathan asked in a shaky whisper.

"Probably." Jem slumped. "It doesn't really matter *who* they are. If they take Silver, we're stranded."

## ⊰ CHAPTER 16 ⊱

# Twists and Turns

Jem crouched behind the tree for a full minute, eyes closed, barely breathing. His heart raced out of control. Without the horse, it would take the rest of the day and well into the night to make their way home, even if they ran all the way. Which they couldn't. Not to mention what came out at night: wolves and mountain lions and—

Jem bit back a yelp when Nathan's hand came down on his shoulder. His eyes flew open. Nathan motioned toward the trail. Cautiously, Jem poked his head out from around the massive trunk. Waves of guilt washed over him as he watched the men untie Silver and lead him away.

*If only I'd stayed home. Silver would be safe.* Never mind that they were stranded. Jem had now lost two of the Coulter horses. He clenched his jaw. *Stop feeling sorry for yourself. Think what to do!*

It was no use. Jem couldn't think of any plan to get them out of this fix. Only one glad thought crossed his mind. *At least Ellie's not here. She's safe at home. Thank you, God, for that turkey.* Pa would only skin him a little for being here. *After he gets done skinning me for losing the rifle, that is. And the horses.*

"I wish we hadn't come," Nathan said, intruding into

Jem's bleak thoughts. He didn't keep his voice down. Silver and the two men were out of sight.

"I'm sorry, Nathan," Jem said. "It was a stupid, *stupid* idea."

"I couldn't agree more," a new voice broke in.

Jem stiffened in shock and whipped around. Less than ten yards away, Rafe stood with his arms crossed, glaring down at the boys with dark, furious eyes.

Jem clutched his cousin's arm. "Run!"

Nathan's face went white. But he leaped to his feet when Jem did and began to run. The boys cut across the side of the hill, away from where they'd seen Silver being led. Jem scanned the forest for hiding places, but bright daylight made ducking into the brush foolish—not with Rafe just steps behind them.

A muffled cry brought Jem to a sudden halt. There could be only one reason for that sound. When he turned around, he saw the worst. Rafe held Nathan in a tight grip. One hand covered his mouth. His cousin's eyes were huge with terror. Jem sagged in defeat.

Without a word, Rafe motioned Jem to follow him. He dragged Nathan to a clump of trees and shoved him to the ground. "Keep quiet, both of you," he ordered in a harsh whisper. "Don't move." He squatted in front of the boys and regarded Jem with a look of annoyance. "What fool notion brought you up here? Do you *want* to get yourselves killed?"

Jem clamped his jaw shut and stared at the ground. *You told us to keep quiet!* Besides, his throat was so tight he couldn't squeeze a word out. He shrugged and focused his attention on a line of ants marching through the pine needles a few inches away.

"That's no answer," Rafe snapped. "Do you think they don't post a lookout? It took no time at all to send somebody to scout around for you." He grunted. "You were lucky to be nowhere near your horse."

Jem's head snapped up. "*They* post a lookout? Don't you mean *we*? You and your night-rider pals?" He clenched his fists to keep from shaking. If only he were a little bigger! If only Nathan had run a little faster!

Rafe's eyebrows shot up. Then he narrowed his eyes. "Keep your smart mouth to yourself, boy. This is not a game. There's no time to explain. We have to go." He stood and beckoned them to follow.

Jem had no intention of following this traitor anywhere. He sat stone-still and glared at the former Pony rider. Nathan sat motionless beside him.

Rafe shook his head, as if he couldn't believe how stupid two boys could be. "I said"—he reached down and jerked Jem roughly to his feet—"let's *go!*"

Jem turned into a fighting, biting wildcat. He kicked and thrashed. "Run, Nathan!" he hollered, just before Rafe's hand locked over Jem's mouth. The young man was not much bigger than Jem, but he was strong and wiry. In less than ten seconds, he had Jem pinned against a tree trunk and was holding him fast.

"Shhh!" Rafe motioned Nathan over.

In the sudden stillness, Jem heard a new sound: shouting. He tried to wriggle loose, but Rafe's grip was like iron.

"Be still," he hissed. "Your fool yelling brought them. I—"

He broke off when a group of men rushed through the trees and headed straight for them.

Jem felt Rafe stiffen. He took his hand from Jem's mouth and reached for his holster. "I didn't mean for it to go like this," he whispered in Jem's ear. "But it's the way it's gotta be for now." He drew his pistol. "Trust me."

Trust Rafe? When he'd just pulled a gun on him? "Not likely," Jem said.

"If you want to get out of this fix in one piece, keep your mouth shut," Rafe warned. He pulled Jem away from the tree, lined him up next to Nathan, and lifted his weapon. "I found these two young pups nosin' around up here," he called to the men.

An older, husky man with stubble for a beard and a mop of graying hair stepped forward. One look at his cold, chiseled face told Jem that here stood the leader of the thieving band.

"Good catch, Rafe." He approached the boys and leaned into their faces "What're ya doin' up here?"

Nathan coughed. Jem winced and stepped back. The man's breath reeked. His clothes stank. Next to this fellow, Strike-it-rich Sam smelled like a rose in full bloom. Jem looked at his boots.

The man swore and cuffed Jem across the head. "Answer me."

The blow caught Jem by surprise. He staggered backward against Rafe, head spinning. Fingers of dread crawled up his spine. *That hurt!* What hurt worse was knowing that he and Nathan were alone. *No, not alone,* he reminded himself firmly. *God is here.*

Rafe righted Jem and shoved him back in place. "Clem has a short fuse," he warned. "Better do like he says."

Jem rubbed the side of his head and considered. Right now, following Rafe's advice looked pretty good. "You t-took my horse from town," he stammered. "I want him back."

"Anything *else?*" Clem mocked with a sneering laugh.

Jem swallowed. "I want Silver back too, and my Pa's rifle and scabbard."

Another smack sent Jem reeling back into Rafe's arms. "Don't get cocky, boy." Clem turned and stalked away. "Bring 'em along," he called over his shoulder.

"But Clem," Rafe argued, "they're a couple o' *kids.* It'll take 'em hours to trudge back to town on foot. Why keep 'em? They'll be nothin' but trouble to watch."

Clem grunted and kept walking. "That's why *you're* watchin' 'em."

Rafe groaned.

The others laughed and took off after their leader.

"Clem doesn't like loose ends getting away," one of the younger men reminded Rafe. "'Specially ones that have seen his face."

"Shut up, Farley."

Farley chuckled and slapped Rafe on the back. "See ya back at the horses."

Rafe holstered his pistol, grabbed each boy by an arm, and hauled them after the returning men. By the time they reached the main trail and the horses, Rafe was breathing fire. "This is one fix you're not getting out of so easily," he muttered, yanking Miwok's reins from a scrub pine.

Farley had remained behind to help tote Clem's "guests" back to camp. He motioned Jem to climb up behind him. Rafe hoisted a white-faced Nathan into the saddle and took off.

Jem held on for dear life as the man in front of him spurred his horse into a dead run. *What's the big hurry?* he wanted to shout, but one look at Rafe galloping beside him reminded Jem to keep his mouth shut.

Ten minutes later, the trail turned in between high canyon walls covered with soaring pines and outcroppings of granite. It twisted and turned like a snake, deeper and deeper into the wilderness. Narrow, rugged side canyons split off in all directions.

The rider barely slowed. He continued to race along the canyon floor as if a mountain lion were after him. Jem clutched Farley's waist and prayed the ride would end soon. A sudden leap over a small gully snapped Jem's neck and made him yell. The horse stumbled, righted itself, then came to an abrupt stop. "Off," Farley barked.

Jem slid to the ground, dazed from his bone-rattling

ride. He glanced around and gulped. Blackwater Canyon spread out before him in all its raw majesty. The canyon was wider here, and part of the floor rose to a broad ledge over-looking Blackwater Creek. The stream splashed over stones the size of Aunt Rose's watermelons. In the distance, jagged openings in the canyon walls branched off into a maze of unexplored gorges, creek beds, and steep cliffs.

Without a word, Jem and Nathan followed Rafe and Farley as they led their horses up onto the rise. Jem spied a crude shack partially hidden behind a stand of stunted pine trees. A fire snapped and crackled nearby. What looked like a suckling pig roasted on a spit over the blaze. Jem's breath quickened. He leaned toward Nathan and whispered, "I wonder whose pig they stole for their feast."

Rafe stopped and turned around. He ripped Jem's hat off and rapped him on the head. "Quiet." Then he plopped the hat back down and hailed Clem, who stood near the fire. "Where do you want 'em?"

"Your problem."

Rafe pressed his lips together and scowled. It was clear he didn't want nanny duty. He shaded his eyes and scanned the area. Then he pointed to a dark crack high in the canyon wall. "Up there, out of the way. Nobody wants to listen to a couple of blubbering boys."

Blubbering boys! Fury made Jem's cheeks blaze, but he cooled off quickly when he saw the dark opening Rafe was pointing out. Clefts in rocky walls, combined with hot August days, meant only one thing: rattlesnake hideouts. "You can't put us—"

A painful pinch stifled Jem's outcry. He rubbed his arm and glared at Rafe. Right now, he hated the former Pony Express rider more than he hated the night riders.

"Do it," Clem ordered. "I'll deal with 'em later, after I get some grub."

Rafe reached into the rifle scabbard buckled to Miwok's saddle. He drew out his rifle and slung it over his shoulder. "Whatever you say, Clem." He didn't look happy.

The path to the cave led past the corral Jem had seen earlier from the canyon's rim. Two dozen fine-looking horses stood around with half-closed eyes. They swished their tails against the unrelenting attack of flies and gnats. A few dug their noses into loose hay scattered in the corners.

A familiar whinny brought Jem up short. His heart leaped. Copper! The chestnut gelding was leaning far out over the railing. Silver stood motionless beside him, watching Jem. Copper nickered again.

Jem lurched forward, but Rafe pulled him back and forced him to keep walking. *I'm sorry, Copper.* A sob caught in his throat, and his shoulders began to shake. *I won't break down. Not in front of Rafe. I'm not a blubbering boy!* He set his jaw and looked away from the corral.

Rafe nudged Jem and Nathan past a wagon piled high with goods, then up a steep, narrow path. When they arrived at the cave's opening, Nathan plopped to the ground and began to scoot inside.

Jem didn't blame him for wanting to escape the sun's glare, but he grabbed his arm. "Don't go in there, Cousin, unless you want snakes for neighbors."

Nathan flung himself backward, scraping his head on the low, rocky overhang. He scuttled away from the cleft like a crab at the seashore. "Snakes? In there?"

"Probably." Jem sat down a safe distance from the cave and picked up a fist-sized rock. He chucked it into the gaping hole and waited.

A loud buzzing sound sent Nathan scurrying father away from the opening.

Jem squinted at Rafe. "But the biggest and most dangerous snake of all is right here."

"You got it wrong, boy," Rafe said. "I stashed you in this out-of-the-way hidey hole for one reason." He leaned closer. "I'm going to get you outta here."

# ⇥ CHAPTER 17 ⇤

# Distant Rumblings

Jem gaped at Rafe. His heart skipped a beat then settled into a dull throbbing that pounded in his ears. Thirty or forty feet below, a dozen men mingled around the fire, laughing and stuffing themselves on roast pork. The only way out of Blackwater Canyon was past those armed night riders. *Who does Rafe think he's fooling?*

"You don't believe me."

Jem shook his head.

Rafe shrugged. "No matter. Let's go."

"*Go?* Go where?" Jem looked up. There might be places along the canyon where the sides were not so steep they couldn't be climbed. But not here. This wall stretched upward at a sharp angle. A mountain goat could probably navigate around those rocks, but not Jem. Or Nathan.

"You're part of that gang down there," Nathan piped up, red-faced and tousled. He'd lost his hat, and blood streaked his pale hair. He glared at Rafe. "Why should we go anywhere with you?"

A new thought chilled Jem clear to his toes. What if Rafe had been ordered to take them deep into the canyon and get rid of them . . . for good? Farley's words slammed into his

128

head. *"Clem doesn't like loose ends getting away. 'Specially ones that have seen his face."*

Jem swallowed. Nathan and he were definitely *loose ends*.

Rafe didn't give Jem time to ponder. He shaded his eyes against the afternoon glare and eyed the activity below. "We have to go *now*, while they're relaxing."

Jem didn't move.

Rafe turned from peering over the ledge and yanked Jem to his feet. "They won't hesitate to kill you both if they think you can identify them. Listen to me. *I am not part of this gang.*"

Jem snorted. "Hang it all, Rafe! Why should I believe you? You *know* them. They know you. And . . . you stole Pa's rifle."

*"What?* Whoa, boy. I never stole your pa's rifle. I needed a rifle, and Clem pointed to the pile. Simple as that." He took a deep breath. "There's a good reason why those skunks down there know me. And why I had to make it look like I was turning you in." He gave Jem a shake. "But there's no time to explain. Trust me. Your lives depend on it."

Jem hesitated. Maybe Rafe was telling the truth. His words sounded sincere. He looked sincere. But then . . . he'd pretended before, back on the ranch. *Dear God, please tell me what to do!*

They could not sneak past the men. They couldn't climb the cliff walls. That left—Jem gulped—going deeper into the canyon to hide. And most likely to wander around in circles until they died of starvation or thirst or wild beasts got them or—

*Lo, I am with you always* . . . A verse he'd learned for the Sunday school contest slipped into Jem's anxious mind. His heart calmed. *God will be with us.* Besides, leaving was better than staying near a nest of snakes—those in the cave, and the two-legged ones below. He bit his lip and looked at Nathan.

Nathan nodded. Snakes were also clearly on his cousin's mind.

"All right," Jem said.

Rafe blew out a breath and shouldered the rifle. "Follow me . . . and *hurry.*"

Hurry, hurry! Rafe's urging took on new meaning as Jem struggled to keep his balance on the rocky path. Every few yards he slipped on loose shale. The clattering of small stones from behind told him that Nathan was having no better luck staying upright. "We're going slower than a blind mule," he muttered to their guide.

"It won't be long before things smooth out," Rafe promised. He led them around a sharp bend, where the gorge narrowed. Steep cliffs and thick stands of pines cut off the sunshine; the path plummeted toward the canyon floor. In the shadows below, Blackwater Creek took on the appearance of its dark name.

Jem shuddered. "Nothing looks smooth here. More like straight down."

Rafe grunted and charged headlong down the hill. "Move!"

It was not smooth, but they did go faster. *Much* faster. Jem and Nathan spent most of the trip down on their backsides. By the time they reached the bottom of the canyon, Jem was sure he'd worn a hole in the seat of his pants. It stung worse than a licking.

No time to rest. No time to snatch a drink from their canteens. Rafe hurried the boys over rocks and around boulders that lay scattered along the creek bed. Jem panted to keep up. "Still not smooth!" he yelled.

Rafe ignored Jem's outburst and waved them on. His destination appeared to be a narrow ravine on the other side of the creek.

*Crack!* Jem flinched and ducked when a bullet struck

the boulder next to him. Rock fragments flew everywhere. Another gunshot sent Jem scurrying for cover. Nathan threw himself down beside Jem, and they crouched behind a large boulder.

"Didn't take 'em long to discover we left," Rafe muttered under his breath. He raised the rifle then paused. "You say this is your pa's?"

Jem nodded.

Rafe thrust the rifle into Jem's hands. "Let 'em know we're not helpless." He yanked both pistols from his holster and sent two shots in the direction they'd come.

Jem's fingers shook, but it felt good to have Pa's rifle back in Coulter hands. When another *crack* sounded, he poked the rifle out from his hiding place. He didn't dare show his face. He made sure the chamber held a cartridge, then he pulled the trigger and hoped for the best. The recoil sent him reeling backward.

Silence greeted Jem's shot. A good thing too. He was shaking so hard he'd dropped the rifle. He couldn't fire it again. He squeezed his eyes shut and pressed closer against the rock.

*They really want to kill us!*

Cold fear numbed Jem's mind. He'd been in scary situations before. Frenchy had planned to dump him in an old mining hole and leave him for dead. Earlier this summer he'd been trapped in the belly of an old mine.

But nobody had ever shot at him before. Until now.

*I should have waited for Pa, even if it meant losing Copper and the rifle.* A sob caught in Jem's throat. *Please, God! I don't want to die.*

Rafe clamped down on his shoulder. Jem gasped, and his eyes flew open. Beside him, Nathan sat frozen.

"There's just two of 'em," Rafe said. "You boys head for that gorge." He pointed out the large opening in the canyon's far wall. "There's plenty of places to hide in there. Don't look back. Take your pa's rifle and *run*." When Jem didn't move, Rafe gave him a shove. "Don't worry, Jem. I'll keep 'em busy."

Jem tried to wrap his mind around Rafe's words. *Run? Leave Rafe behind?*

He gripped his father's heavy rifle. Jem didn't know why Rafe was with these night riders, but he suddenly knew the pony rider was telling the truth. *He's not part of that gang!* Jem's head cleared. He felt trust replace fear. He would trust that God knew Rafe's heart and would use him to save their lives.

"I have about eight shots left, so don't dawdle," Rafe said. "I'll follow when I can. Just stay put once you find a hiding place. You don't want to get lost back there." He grinned at Jem's stricken look. "Don't worry, I can track you, so long as you don't wander too far." He peered over the top of the boulder and fired. "Go!"

New fear—a healthy fear—surged through Jem's veins. He leaped over rocks, stumbled, scrambled up, and ran some more, with Nathan close behind. He sloshed through shallow Blackwater Creek without looking back.

Jem kept ahead of Nathan, in spite of the nine-pound rifle he was lugging. Two . . . three . . . four . . . He counted Rafe's shots and judged the distance to the ravine. "We're almost there!" he called to Nathan, chancing a quick look back. He heard two more shots. *Please take care of Rafe,* he prayed on the run.

A minute later, the boys ducked into the narrow canyon mouth. Jem paused to consider their next move. Plenty of places to hide, Rafe had said. Jem agreed. Numerous gullies, draws, and a dry creek bed opened before them. Trees and rocky outcroppings covered the sides. Best of all, the slope was not too steep to climb.

Nathan stopped to rest beside Jem. His shoulders heaved with the effort to catch his breath. "Are we . . . safe now?"

Another shot rang out. Jem hoped it was Rafe's and not a night rider's. "No. C'mon."

They left the canyon floor and staggered along a deer trail that led up the hill. The late afternoon sun soon dipped behind the cliff tops, plunging everything into shadows. Twilight fell early in Blackwater Canyon, and with it came a chilly mountain breeze.

The boys stopped partway up to rest near a cluster of jagged granite rocks and tall pines. It looked like a good hiding place. Plus, Jem could see the opening to the gorge from here, and along a good portion of it as well. The ravine cut a dark ribbon deeper into the mountains.

"How much farther into this creepy canyon do we have to go?" Nathan asked.

"No farther," Jem said. As far as he was concerned, they'd come too far already. Strike's stories of lost prospectors swirled in his memory. He fixed his gaze on the way out. "As long as we stay put, we won't get lost. We can follow the creek bed back. It's only when you wander around too long that you get confused and lose your way." He shivered.

"For how long?"

Jem frowned. "Until Rafe comes. There's plenty of cover. We can watch from here."

"What if"—Nathan drew a deep breath—"what if he doesn't come?"

Jem didn't want to think about that. Rafe would come. He had to. "I'm sure a Pony Express rider is used to getting out of scrapes. He'll find a way." But a gruesome picture came to mind: Rafe lying on the rocks—injured or dead.

Jem didn't share his thoughts with Nathan. Instead, he gave a shaky laugh. "Your ma is gonna skin us alive."

Nathan didn't laugh.

Twilight grew deeper. The stars came out. Still no Rafe. No shots either, but that didn't mean it was over. Jem strained to see through the gloom then sat back and scooted closer to his cousin. In the distance, several flashes lit up the sky above the high Sierra. The light was followed by a faint rumbling.

Nathan nudged him. "What's that?"

"I don't know." Jem looked up. "It can't be a storm. It's a clear night."

A few more flashes made Jem frown in thought, but he shrugged it off when he didn't hear more thunder. If it *was* a summer storm, it was far away from here.

The evening passed eerily quiet. The earlier breeze died away. No coyotes yipped. No water gurgled through the dry creek bed below. Then Jem heard it again—a faint, distant rumbling. "It sure sounds like thunder," he said. "But it can't be. The sky's full of stars."

The rumbling grew louder. Jem stood up. A prickling in the back of his mind made his spine tingle. *Something's not right.*

"It's coming from the gorge," Nathan said. "It sounds like water."

*Water?* "Oh, no!" How often had Strike told stories of cloudbursts in the high country? The canyons below stayed dry as dust until a summer storm dumped its load up in the mountains. Water would soon spill down this narrow ravine, thirty or forty feet deep. Maybe even deeper. The night riders kept their camp up on that ledge for a reason.

"We gotta go!" Jem grabbed the rifle and scrambled for higher ground.

## CHAPTER 18

# Night Dangers

Nathan asked no questions. He sprang up and followed on Jem's heels. Teeth chattering in terror, Jem groped his way up the ridge. It was getting so dark he had to feel for each step. In his hurry, he slipped on loose gravel, fell, and plowed backward into Nathan. The rifle slid from his grasp.

Nathan yelped and went sprawling. He caught the rifle with one hand as it clattered past. Panting, he lay flat against the ground while rocks and small pieces of gravel rolled by.

"Thanks, Cousin." Jem took the rifle and kept climbing. The rumbling had turned to a dull roar, like a waterfall. Jem couldn't see the wall of water, but he could feel moisture in the air, even from halfway up the hill.

"How much higher?" Nathan wheezed.

"The higher, the better." No longer did Jem worry about losing his way in this canyon's maze. Nor was he afraid that a wolf, cougar, or another wild beast might get him. The thought of being swept away by the churning water spurred him upward. Blindly, he crawled the rest of the way to the top of the ridge then collapsed. His legs felt like jelly.

Nathan fell to the ground beside him, breathing hard. Finally, he asked, "What is it?"

"A flash flood," Jem said between breaths. "We're safe up here." *Please, God, let us be safe up here!* Far below, raging water thundered through the narrow channel. It would soon meet up with Blackwater Creek and roar through the main canyon. "I hope Rafe found high ground."

Darkness had now fallen completely, except for the milky band of stars that stretched out over Jem's head. He didn't dare move from where he and Nathan huddled against a massive, broken-off tree trunk. The outline of mountains showed a solid wall of black all around them. Deep chasms might be only a dozen steps away.

"We're not going anywhere tonight," Jem said. "It's too dark. In the morning we can work our way back."

"Back to the gang's hideout?"

Jem buried his face in his hands. Nathan was right. If Rafe didn't come for them, how would they get out of this canyon alive? Try to find their way and get hopelessly turned around like all those other prospectors? Or walk back into the night riders' camp?

"Not much of a choice," he muttered.

"Huh?"

"Nothing," Jem said, sighing. "But at least we don't have to stay in the dark all night." From his pocket, he pulled out his two most prized possessions: his pocketknife and a tin of matches.

Nathan gave him a worried look. "They might see a fire way up here."

Jem shook his head. "We'll keep it hidden, and it's too dark to see any smoke."

There was plenty of dead wood and dry pine needles nearby. In no time, the boys had cleared a patch of ground behind a rocky outcropping and kindled a small, hot fire. The cheery blaze raised Jem's spirits as much as if it had been high noon.

Nathan's spirits clearly rose too. His eyes glowed from across the fire. He spread his hands out and scooted closer to the warmth. "I never thought I'd say this, but you know what, Jem? This could be a lot worse. It's not like the awful night we spent in the mine."

Jem shuddered in grim memory. "You're right. Nothing could be as bad as waking up in the pitch black, trapped under solid rock." He gazed up at the vast expanse of stars, happy to be out in the open.

Then reality hit. They were not trapped underground, but they were still trapped. What would they do in the morning? The water in their canteens wouldn't last forever. Jem listened. The roar from below had faded to a shallow splashing. Cloudbursts spilled their rain and were over—just like that. The ravine would soon run dry again. Without water, they'd be forced to return to the main canyon and Blackwater Creek.

*Not a good idea,* he told himself. But at least they were safe for now. "Rafe won't try to find us tonight. It's too dark for even an Indian scout to track us, and our fire is hidden pretty good. I say we take turns keeping our eyes open and the fire burning. Just in case."

Nathan's eyebrows shot up. "In case of what?"

"I dunno." When Nathan pressed him, Jem shrugged. "Night dangers."

"Worse than what we just went through?"

*Yeah, worse.* Night dangers had terrifying names like bear, wolf, bobcat, or cougar. If Nathan couldn't figure that out, Jem wasn't going to say it aloud. He propped Pa's rifle across his knees and yawned. "You try to sleep. I'll take the first watch. When I can't keep my eyes open any longer, I'll wake you."

Nathan shuffled around, trying to get comfortable. He ended up a few feet from the fire, curled into a ball, his eyes squeezed shut. He did not look at all restful.

Jem wriggled and twisted against the stump, trying to find a smooth place for his back. It was going to be a long night. He tossed a small branch on the fire and watched sparks leap into the air. He followed them with his eyes until they blinked out. Then he looked up and saw the stars. It made him feel a little tingly, seeing the stars so close. It made God feel close too.

"Maybe counting stars will keep me awake," he murmured. Then he chuckled. There were too many stars to count. He remembered how Strike had laughed once on a prospecting trip, when a much younger Jem had set out to count every star. *"God makes 'em faster than you can count 'em, young'un."*

Maybe He did. It sure seemed like new stars popped out the instant Jem started counting. *This feels almost like a prospecting trip. If I keep thinking I'm camping with Strike or Pa, I can make it through the night.*

Jem yawned and stopped counting stars. No scary noises made his heart flutter. The snap of a branch or an occasional coyote's cry might have kept Jem awake. He might have even made good on his promise to wake Nathan when he couldn't keep his eyes open any longer.

Instead, he fell asleep.

A quick, light tapping on his arm brought Jem around. Dark had lifted enough to see Nathan sitting so close he was practically in Jem's lap. The rifle had slipped to his side and lay on the ground next to him. Two feet away, the fire was barely smoldering. A thin wisp of smoke curled above the embers.

Nathan's drumbeat tapping turned into a grip that nearly caused Jem to yelp. His cousin's eyes looked huge and scared. Jem shifted in place, but Nathan shook his head and held him still. With his free hand, he pointed across the fire.

Jem looked . . . and caught his breath. Several yards away, standing as still as statues, two large wolves stared back at the boys. Jem felt the blood drain from his face. He didn't move a muscle, although his thoughts were screaming, *Run, run!*

Jem knew better than to give the wolves something to chase. He peeled Nathan's fingers from his arm and waited. Maybe the pair were out for a morning stroll and just passing by. *And maybe they have a den of pups and need a quick and easy meal.* Jem swallowed that horrifying thought.

"The rifle," Nathan whispered in his ear. "Can you get it?"

Jem nodded. Pa's rifle was touching his leg. Here was a chance to get the wolf that "got away" last week. Inch by inch, Jem allowed his fingers to creep down his leg until he felt the cold metal of the rifle barrel. Slowly, he lifted the gun to his lap.

The wolves didn't seem to notice. They continued to play their watch-and-see game with the boys. An eerie feeling wormed its way into Jem's thoughts. Who would "blink" first? *What are they waiting for?* He lifted the rifle higher, quietly clicked a round into place, and took aim.

"Shoot 'em," Nathan hissed.

Jem had every intention of shooting at least one of them. Then he paused. They weren't doing anything. They stood there with the quiet patience of a forest hunter. Were they waiting for Jem to make the first move?

Uncertainty flooded his mind. He was pretty sure neither of these wolves had killed Pepper. If one of them had, he'd have shot it without a second's thought. But twenty miles was a long way for a hungry wolf to go to pick a fight with a rancher. This pair looked sleek and well-fed. It was a good bet they had a family holed up somewhere close by.

*Can I shoot a wolf just for looking at me?*

Jem drew a deep breath and made his decision. He pointed Pa's rifle in the air and sent four shots flying high. The wolves took off across the ridge and disappeared into the woods before the last *crack* of the rifle shot faded away.

## CHAPTER 19

# Surprises

**H**ang it all!" Jem dropped the rifle and rubbed his left hand against the side of his britches. Four quick shots had heated the Henry's metal barrel and made it too hot to hold. Pa's warning about that came back in a flash, but it was too late now. His hand stung. One shot probably would have worked just as well. *But I wanted those wolves gone!*

"Are you all right?" Nathan asked, gulping back his surprise.

Jem stood up and used his boot to scrape dirt across the remains of the campfire. "I'm fine. Just dumb." He scooped up his canteen, took a swallow of water, and shouldered it. Then he gingerly picked up the rifle by its wood stock, careful to stay away from the still-hot barrel.

Nathan looked puzzled. "Where are we going?"

"Back to our first hiding place. We can see the whole ravine from there. The flash flood most likely washed away our tracks, so Rafe might need a little help finding us. If we spot him, we can holler at him." Jem's look turned grim. "Somebody else might've heard the shots. If we see anybody but Rafe, we can sneak away deeper into the canyon and hide."

By the time the boys crept back to the granite outcropping they'd hidden behind the day before, the sun had risen in a blaze of glory. No trace of last evening's watery wall remained in the creek bed. Jem briefly wondered how the night riders' camp had fared.

He shook his canteen and sighed. "It's gonna be a long—"

A faint *yoo-hoo* suddenly echoed through the canyon. It bounced from one side to the other, then disappeared.

Jem dived behind the outcropping. Nathan slammed into him in his hurry to find cover. "Who is it?" he asked.

"I don't know." Jem peeked over the ledge. Far below, four men were cautiously making their way along the creek bank. The water had disappeared, but the rocks looked slippery as soap. The men were skidding and tripping all over the place. Finally, the tall man in the lead stopped and cupped his hands to his mouth.

"*Yoo-hoo!* Jem! Nathan! Are you here?"

Jem wrinkled his forehead in confusion. It wasn't Rafe. And as far as he knew, the night riders didn't know his name. He squinted hard, trying to make out who it was. Then he gasped. "Pa?"

Jem leaped to his feet. If it hadn't been for the precious rifle, he would have flown down the treacherous hill head-first. Instead, he clutched the rifle and minded his footing, but he still landed on his backside once or twice. Dust rose in clouds when he tripped and slid a dozen yards. Would he never reach the bottom of the ravine?

Nathan trailed behind at a much slower pace. He kept his footing better and arrived cleaner than Jem, who was covered from head to toe in fine, gray dust. "Uncle Matt!" Nathan shouted and waved.

Pa engulfed Jem in a hug that threatened to cut off his breath. The dirt and filth didn't faze him. A minute later, he grabbed Nathan with his free hand and buried his head in his nephew's hair. "Thank God," he whispered. "Thank God you boys are all right."

Jem didn't let go, even when Pa backed away a few steps. His father sat down right there at the bottom of the hill and pulled Jem and Nathan down beside him. "Let's rest a bit before—"

"Before you tan our hides," Jem mumbled, eyes squeezed shut. "Mine, mostly."

Pa paused. "I meant to say, 'before we hike back,' but if you prefer a licking, I can oblige you. The two of you have most likely given Rosie a severe case of the vapors. Don't know if she'll recover enough to ever let you leave the yard again."

Jem cringed. He didn't know if Pa was teasing. Probably not. Jem pretended to rest, but his thoughts were tied in knots. He didn't know where to begin to explain the mess he'd gotten himself—and Nathan—into. A simple "I'm sorry" could not erase the black marks written all over his actions, starting with that . . . that *pesky wolf!*

When Jem finally opened his eyes, Pa was looking at him. His face was crinkled with worry wrinkles, but he was smiling. "I hear tell it's been a long week."

Jem ducked his head. Tears stung his eyes, but he took a deep breath and held them back. He nodded. *Some man of the family I turned out to be.* He was too ashamed to say it out loud.

A rattling noise brought Jem's head up. Pa had dragged the rifle across the ground and was examining it. "Doesn't look any worse for wear," he remarked. "I hear it got stolen, but I see you got it back for me. Thanks, Son. I'd hate to do without my Henry." He paused. "And you didn't give up until you discovered what happened to Copper, though that didn't turn out exactly as you planned."

"Pa, I—" Jem let out a breath. He didn't know what to say. Pa didn't sound angry. Who had told him all this?

"Granted, going this far into the high country was not your smartest decision," Pa added. "But you were in good hands with Rafe."

Jem's eyes opened wide. In his joy of greeting Pa, he'd forgotten all about Rafe. "Where is he, Pa? He lied to us. To me, to Nathan, and even to Aunt Rose and Ellie. He had your rifle, so I thought he was part of the night—"

"I told you I'm not part of that gang!" Rafe's shout rose from behind Pa. He came around and squatted in front of Jem and Nathan. He looked miserable. His face was scratched. Bruises covered both cheeks. "Listen to me, boy. Didn't I save your life? I barely made it out of that canyon myself." He waved his scratched and bleeding hands in front of Jem's face. "I told you there was a good reason I was with them."

"You're right," Jem said, shaking his head. "I'm sorry. Why were you with them?"

Rafe made himself comfortable next to Pa and gave him a questioning look.

Pa shrugged. "Sure, we got time."

"This gang of night riders has been causing trouble up and down the Mother Lode country for the past year and a half," Rafe explained. "They're ruthless, and have no regard for folks' lives or property." He narrowed his eyes. "They steal horses, weapons, anything they can get their hands on. They murder folks, Jem, then they scurry back to hide in their holes and move on—like rats."

Jem shuddered. He believed it.

"I've been on special assignment with the governor's office to track them down and somehow 'join' their band." He held up his hand when Jem opened his mouth. "I did it. They accepted me, but in order to keep their trust, I had to do things I'm not proud of."

Rafe paused and looked away. "I'll have to reconcile that with God in my own way." Then he continued. "When the gang holed up in Blackwater Canyon, I knew we could finally catch them. Your pa's reputation has spread far and wide since he took over the job of sheriff."

Jem's mouth dropped open. "Pa's?"

Rafe nodded. "I was told to get in touch with Sheriff Coulter of Goldtown. He'd help round up the night riders and end this once and for all. That's what I was doing when I was crossing your range, Jem. But I didn't know the sheriff was out of town. First chance I got, I slipped away and sent him a telegram." He scratched his chin. "I heard that the deputies wired him too, but by that time, he was already on his way home."

"Why didn't you tell us?" Jem asked in a small voice. He'd not only shot a Pony Express hero, he'd shot a *lawman*. Worse and worse!

"In our business," Pa put in, "a loose tongue can get a man killed. Rafe figured it was best to keep quiet, especially since I wasn't around."

"It would've worked just fine," Rafe said with a chuckle, "if I hadn't picked up the wrong rifle from the pile and then brought Ellie that turkey. You put two and two together, Jem. Too bad you couldn't have waited just one more day before taking off to spy on the night riders."

"We just wanted to get proof the thieves were here, Uncle Matt," Nathan spoke up for Jem. "We never planned on sticking around."

Pa nodded. "I know. No-luck and Dakota gave me an earful about what was going on in town. Between their report and Rafe's telegram, and then finding you boys missing, I pieced it together." He grinned. "I deputized half of Goldtown. Last evening we surprised the night riders. The flood was the icing on the cake."

Jem's heart leaped. "You rounded them up? Copper's safe? And Silver? And all the rest?"

Pa reached out and ruffled Jem's hair—his way of telling Jem that everything was all right. "Yep. The thieves who survived the shoot-out are on their way to Goldtown's jailhouse. Other temporary deputies are recovering the loot." He whistled. "It was quite an operation."

Jem let go and relaxed completely. Pa was home; Copper and Silver were safe. Rafe wasn't lying dead in the creek bed. Best of all, Pa didn't seem angry to find Jem in the thick of things. "Now that you caught the thieves, what will you do?" Jem asked Rafe.

Rafe opened his mouth to answer, but Pa cut in. "Actually, I offered Rafe a job. The miners do all right in a pinch, but I need a reliable deputy. If Rafe likes the town and the people, why, I might even consider working myself out of a job some day."

"And . . . ?" Jem held his breath. If Rafe stuck around, just think of the Pony Express stories he could tell! Ellie would jump for joy at that.

The Pony rider shrugged. "I've got some business to settle in Sacramento, but I told your pa I might be back when I'm finished." He smiled at Jem.

Jem couldn't ask for more than that. Now that Rafe wasn't a dirty traitor any longer, he'd returned to his place as one of Jem's heroes. It felt good. He smiled back. "I'd like that."

Pa slapped Jem's knee. "We better get going. It's a *long* ride back to the ranch. And the high country is not to be traveled carelessly."

Jem nodded. "I'm sorry I messed things up, Pa. I just wanted to—" His voice choked.

"To be the man of the family," Pa finished. "I know. And you did good, going after that wolf. Too bad you didn't get him. Do you know what that means, Son?"

*Yeah. I can never be trusted to take over again.* He didn't say it out loud.

When Jem didn't answer, Pa grinned. "It means you and I have to go after that critter. And Nathan too, if he wants."

Jem gaped at his father. "Really?"

Pa winked. "You bet. And maybe, if we ask real nice, Rafe will agree to go along with us before he heads back to Sacramento."

"I reckon I better," Rafe agreed with a chuckle. "That way I can make sure I'm behind the rifle barrel this time, instead of in front of it."

"Well then, what are we waiting for?" Jem leaped to his feet. Pa laughed, and together the group headed down the canyon for home.

# Historical Note

Thomas "Rafe" Flynn is a created character for this story, but the real Thomas Flynn was one of two hundred Pony Express riders who carried the mail from April 1860 until October 1861. Upon accepting the job, each rider received a small, leather-bound Bible, two pistols to ward off dangers along the route, and a *mochila*, a leather saddle covering that could hold twenty pounds of mail. The riders also took this oath:

*"While I am in the employ of A. Majors, I agree not to use profane language, not to get drunk, not to gamble, not to treat animals cruelly and not to do anything else that is incompatible with the conduct of a gentleman. And I agree, if I violate any of the above conditions, to accept my discharge without any pay for my services."*

Telegraphed messages from back East—like the news that Abraham Lincoln had won the 1860 presidential election—were wired to St. Joseph, Missouri. From there, a string of riders carried the written news in less than ten days to Sacramento, California.

The route covered 2,000 miles of plains, deserts, mountains, and rivers. Each rider rode at a full gallop (ten miles per hour) for about one hundred miles. He stopped every eight to ten miles at a way station only long enough to toss his *mochila* onto a fresh horse.

It was a dangerous route, and Indian attacks and buffalo stampedes were only some of the worries. If a horse tripped in a hole, the rider could be thrown and killed. Frightful storms on the plains and blizzards in the mountains made weather the worst danger. Rafe's story of surviving a snow-storm in the Sierra was the true experience of another Pony rider, William Fisher.

The Pony Express operated only eighteen months, but the young riders were heroes for braving the dangers of the West. In October 1861, the telegraph connected Omaha, Nebraska, with Sacramento, California. This new era of faster communication made the Express riders obsolete. After the Civil War, the Pony Express was sold to the Wells Fargo Company, an express, stagecoach, and banking service that is still in business today.

*A Pony Express westbound postmark*
*1860*

Visit www.GoldtownAdventures.com to download a free literature guide with the enrichment activities for *Canyon of Danger.*

# About the Author

Susan K. Marlow is a twenty-year homeschooling veteran and the author of the Circle C Adventures and Circle C Beginnings series. She believes the best part about writing historical adventure is tramping around the actual sites. Although Susan owns a real gold pan, it hasn't seen much action. Panning for gold is a *lot* of hard work. She prefers to combine her love of teaching and her passion for writing by leading writing workshops and speaking at young author events.

You can contact Susan at susankmarlow@kregel.com.

# FOLLOW JEM AND HIS SISTER, ELLIE!

**Twelve-year-old Jem stumbles into exciting adventures in the Goldtown Adventures series**

*Badge of Honor • Tunnel of Gold*
*Canyon of Danger • River of Peril*